QUEEN OF LUST

DESTINY DIESS

Front cover image by Lena B. Wolf.

Editing by: Zainab M., Heart Full of Reads Editing Services

Beta reading by: Kayla Lutz and Madi

Destiny Diess

destinydiess@gmail.com

❀ Created with Vellum

To Sean.

Thank you for believing in me.

CHAPTER 1

I never thought killing would feel so good.

Sitting on the Lust throne, toying with the tines of my ruby-red crown, licking the blood off the corner of my swollen lips, I reveled in the chaos around me with a smile on my face. Demons from Wrath, Envy, Greed, and Pride hurried out of the vast colosseum toward the portal, trampling each other and scurrying away from me in pure, agonizing fear.

Black mist danced around the ruby crown, my maroon painted fingernails drifting through the haze. Maybe it was the angel inside of me who loved seeing demon carcasses littered on the marble floors, or maybe it was my demon who bathed in the feeling of swelling terror. But all I could feel was immense pleasure rushing through my veins and a desire for more blood, more bodies, and especially more souls.

The souls of the demonic wicked that I unapologetically inhaled clawed at my insides, talons cutting into my cold, dark heart, trying to puncture it, trying to tear me down. But nothing could destroy me now.

Everything I believed it, everyone I loved was either dead or had been hurt.

Now wasn't the time to give into wailing demons who I killed.

I shut my eyes softly and inhaled the sweet aroma of decaying bodies, smelling almost everyone's scent under my pink Lust sun except my favorite scent of cinnamon. My chest tightened at the thought of Eros actually leaving. When I told him to get out of here to stay safe, I thought, at least he'd stick around within a few hundred meters of the colosseum to stop me from killing everyone in sight.

But I smelled nothing.

Did he, like Lucifer, want me to lose control? Maybe he wanted to see just how strong I was too. And I knew that if I devoured more meaningless demon souls, I could become the most powerful demon in all of Hell.

When I brushed my fingers across my family ring, I was suddenly brought back down to reality. No... Eros was gone because I told him to protect the last few people I cared about: Dr. U and Jasmine. Killing more souls wouldn't make me stronger. I couldn't do it.

Though I wanted to.

Setting my crown upon my soft brown hair, I sat up and gazed around the marble colosseum. While others screamed in terror, Biast sat five feet away from me with a body in his hands and his fangs sunk deep into someone's neck. He had transformed into a true Wrath demon with eyes swimming in blood; horns longer, thicker, and curvier than moments ago; and a red aura exuding from his red skin.

After sucking as much blood out of the poor caracasses as he could, he let them slip from his talons, sat back, and chuckled wickedly to himself. He lifted his gaze to meet mine, the intense malicious look inside them making me suck in a breath. Claws piercing through the man's throat, he ripped a sheet of his skin apart and sunk his hand into the body, soaking it in blood. "Come here, Dani," Biast snarled.

Unable to resist his command, I found myself slipping from the throne and onto my knees, crawling to him in a haze of lust. *"Give me control, Dani,"* Javier, Biast's dead brother, whispered in the back of my mind at the mere scent of blood. Ignoring him, I knelt beside him and pulled Biast's hand from the body, admiring how the blood rolled down his forearm.

Harshly, Biast snapped his large calloused hard around my throat and squeezed. I inhaled sharply and grabbed his wrist, but I didn't push him away. A wave of pleasure rushed through me, heat gathering in my core. He strummed his fingers across my throat and pulled me closer, pressing his lips back onto mine, the irony taste of blood slipping into my mouth and consuming me.

"Control," Javier said again, but this time he was so distant, so utterly far from my consciousness that I barely heard him. Hundreds, if not thousands, of souls begged for control, taunted me, spoke so loudly that I could barely think straight.

I was sure there were more voices inside of me than demons that I had killed. But how could I feel or hear them? Was it some kind of sorcery? Could I feel the demons and people that *they* had killed before I slaughtered them?

Memories that certainly weren't mine flooded through my mind, the first of a man lying on a dirty wooden floor, clutching a cracked picture frame. Inside the frame was an image of a naked woman tied up and mutilated. Rage rushing through me, I sank my claws into the man's chest and pulled out his heart, his squirming body turning into nothing but a corpse.

Shifting my focus to another soul's memory, I found myself pointing a gun at a bank teller, forcing her to open the back vault and shovel money into my duffle bag, the scent of fresh and filthy dough giving me a rush of adrenaline.

Both satisfying and terrifying thoughts these demons experienced flashed before me. They were so loud in my head that I almost couldn't think straight. But as Biast's rough lips moved against mine and his wet fingers trailed up my gown, they quieted.

Until the red eyes of Mom's killer flashed in my head.

Through the memory of another demon, I watched the red-eyed woman climb on top of a young human woman and draw a knife across her chest and carve out her heart. The demon screamed at her to stop, not to touch the woman he loved, to take him instead, but the heartless red-eyed killer only stopped when she had finished the job, had pulled out the heart, and had consumed it entirely in one enormous bite.

I shoved Biast away, my chest tightening, and sucked in a sharp breath. Whoever she was, I needed to find her as soon as possible. I was Queen of Lust now. I had taken care of everyone who wanted to openly defy me. I was close to being invincible. Now was the time to avenge Mom.

After stumbling to my feet, I walked around the maze of bodies to Lucifer who sat alone, the other commanders' golden thrones vacant. He sipped on his glass of Vemon and drank in the madness with a smile on his face, like this was all his doing. And maybe it was.

"You really outdid yourself this time, Dani," Lucifer said, lifting his icy blue gaze to mine. He tilted his head to swallow the red of his drink and grazed an iced-horn across the chair, the gold glinting against it. "To be feared by even the strongest of demons is the second greatest feeling you'll experience in Hell."

"And the first?" I asked.

Lucifer stood and placed his cup down on the chair. "The first is how you feel when even Mother, that heavenly woman in the sky, is so terrified of you that she rips off your wings and banishes you down here forever."

My lips curled into a smile, and I glanced over my shoulder at the other commanders huddled together by the colosseum entrance. Even Sathanus had cowered away from me today. I would never know the feeling of Mother exiling me, but now I knew that my powers far exceeded Sathanus's or else he would've tried to kill me right in the center of this ten-story arena in front of thousands of demons.

"Don't get too arrogant now, Dani," Lucifer said, studying my face.

"Says the most prideful man in Hell."

Lucifer chuckled, the sound chilling right down to my very bones. "We have a war ahead against the angels that we must prepare for, because the Beginning of the End is here, the prophecy has begun. Death will reign upon us all."

"Beliel's prophecy," I whispered, brows furrowing slightly. "But how do you know?"

"Look around," Lucifer said. "It's the 18th day of the twenty-fifth year of this century. Bodies are littered around us, Biast is drinking their blood, and—"

"And their souls are bound to me," I said, my stomach turning into knots.

If this was truly the beginning of the end, then Hell was about to rise from the ashes, and war with Mother was about to commence sooner than I hoped. We weren't prepared, at least I wasn't. Not when I wanted to kill the red-eyed woman and couldn't control my urges for souls.

A rightful wave of guilt washed over me. I needed to find Eros, Dr. U, and Jasmine, because I had some explaining to do and a lot of shit to make up for. I nearly killed both Eros and Jasmine tonight, and Dr. U—the only family I really had left—had almost died because of me.

Placing a hand on my back, Lucifer guided me to the colosseum exit. Huddled in a circle, the commanders chatted quietly until we walked over. Envy crossed her arms across her chest and strummed her mint-colored acrylic nails on her elbow. While she had that usual envious look on her face, I could see the fear deep in her eyes and could smell a salty and sweaty stench drifting off her.

Greed stood beside her with one hand on her golden-clad hip, eyes trembling when she looked in my direction. She tugged on some pearl earrings and quickly looked back at Envy, as if she was unsure glancing at me would piss me off again.

Sathanus stood with his fists clenched by his side and his eyes completely red balls of fire, hatred and anger spewing from his sanguine-colored lips and—what looked to be—steam fuming from his ears.

And the good 'ole Sloth and Gluttony commanders refused to make eye contact with me but both munched on some Fervor Crisps that were supposed to be for the after-party. Though it didn't seem like any other demons wanted to party after now. The colosseum and castle had cleared out, demons running down the white stone paths to Chastion, the nearest town.

"Not at all what we expected from this crowning ceremony," Envy stated boldly, the first commander to say a single word to me.

"I didn't expect two Envies to nearly murder my family," I said, grinding my fangs together. "And I certainly didn't expect one of those Envies to have been friends with me, *Commander*. It all seemed a bit too… coincidental, don't you think?"

Envy glared at me with emerald green eyes, similar to Kasey's. Instead of cowering back in fear like I used to, I stared back at her twice as hard until she grumbled under her breath and looked away from me.

"Now is not the time to make accusations, Queen," Greed said, straightening out her back and glancing at Lucifer. "We shall set a time to officially meet and talk about what happened, because killing innocent lives cannot be tolerated."

"Innocent?" Lucifer laughed. "Dani was challenged, and she stepped up and proved herself. There is nothing intolerable about that. Unless, you believe that Dani has accumulated too much power, and for that, I *kindly* tell you to fuck off."

Trying my best to suppress a smirk, I cleared my throat. "We will meet on Sunday morning when the Lust sun is highest in the air, but my crowning will not be the topic of conversation." I paused, my stomach tightening again. "A war is approaching, a war with the angels."

Sathanus barked out an empty laugh. "War with angels? Are you still going on about that prophecy, Lucifer? You know that shit isn't real. It's made-up shit that Mother whispered into Beliel's ear before she fucking banished her."

"Made-up like your religion?" Lucifer asked, arching a platinum blond brow and clasping his hands behind his back. "Didn't you just make Satanism up, so your subjects blindly follow you? Or was that someone else?"

An unruly growl exited Sathanus's mouth. "Fucking watch it, Lucifer."

"Or what?" Lucifer challenged.

When Sathanus lunged in our direction, Lucifer grabbed his forearm, stopping him completely, and shoved him back. I stepped between them and stared pointedly at Sathanus. "Be here at noon on Sunday. Don't be late."

This wasn't the time to fight, because fighting led to soul-sucking madness. And, God, if I started again, I didn't think I'd be able to stop. I had killed so many demons and felt nothing but a nagging numbness and a deep, plaguing fear that something much worse was coming.

My mind might've now been haunted by thousands of demons, but the beginning of the end was here, and we had to be ready for the worst. It was our time to rise, our time to rule, and *my time* to kill Mother for betraying Mom and letting her die in the hands of the red-eyed woman.

CHAPTER 2

Following the sweet scent of cinnamon up my white marble steps, I wandered down the halls and to one of the many spare rooms Eros and I had in the castle. On my way up here, I had come up with a thousand and one things I wanted to say to everyone I cared about. But now, standing in front of the closed door, I couldn't seem to open my mouth.

Deciding that I'd wing it, I took a deep breath, pushed open the door, and gazed at a beaten and bruised Dr. U who laid in the canopy bed. Eros stood over her, brushing some strands of Dr. U's graying blonde hair off her face. When I cleared my throat, Eros looked over his shoulder and blew out a deep breath, his piercing emerald eyes softening. "Thank the fucking heavens you're okay."

I closed the door behind me and gave him a small smile, knowing that now wasn't the time to embrace him after everything I had done. While my hunger had been satisfied, I had just hurt and killed so many people. Part of me thought I didn't deserve the pure adoration he gave me every waking moment.

But, despite my inclination to stay away, all I wanted to do was run into his arms, bury my face into his chest, and lie with him in our bed to forget it all and to thank him for helping me become stronger. If I hadn't gotten stronger, we all would've died, and Maeve would've been ruling Lust by now.

Eros extended a hand out of me, his brown hair parted to the side. I smiled a bit wider at him and intertwined my fingers with his, finally allowing myself to relax beside him in his cinnamon aroma. I rested my head on his shoulder and looked over at Jasmine who sat by a large glass window, probably staring down at all the people hurrying out of Lust.

She didn't look at me, and I didn't blame her.

This was all my fault. I let this get out of hand, hurt people, scared people, endangered them even. If someone didn't stop me, I could've devoured Jasmine and not have given a damn at the time. I wouldn't be surprised if Jasmine wanted to go back to Earth and work at the Lounge again, instead of living with us.

What I feared the most was that Jasmine would never want to be friends again. She was the only other person besides Eros that I had down here, and I didn't want her to leave too. But if she did, then I had nobody else to blame except myself. I drove her away, whether I meant to or not.

After forcing myself to pull my gaze away, I hesitantly walked over to Dr. U's bedside and knelt next to her, taking her shredded hand between both of mine and silently praying that these injuries would heal and that she wouldn't die on me.

It hadn't been less than a couple hours since I last saw her, and she already looked worse. I wanted her better as soon as possible, so she could get back to what she loved doing—helping people figure out their lives and guiding young interns like I was onto a better path for the future.

If she was awake, she wouldn't want to be in Hell with me.

"Has she woken up yet?" I asked, softly.

Dr. U stirred and shifted her bandaged face toward me,

opening her swollen eyes as far as she could. "Dani," she said, voice dry and scratchy like nails on a chalkboard. She weakly squeezed my hand and mewled in pain.

"Someone get her water, please," I said.

Jasmine disappeared into the hallway, the door clicking closed behind her, and returned a few moments later with a glass of water. I took it from her, my fingers brushing against her slightly, and placed it against Dr. U's lips, like she used to give me antidepressant medication after Mom died.

She drank it willingly, then pushed it away. "Thank you."

"The doctor will be back soon for you." I gently glided my fingers across Dr. U's bandages and cursed at myself for everything that happened. Every bruise, every scratch, every fucking hair pulled out of her head was because of me being an angel and leading one of the most powerful kingdoms in all of Hell.

Dr. U pulled my hands away from her face. "Are you okay, Dani?"

While I wanted to assure her that everything was fine, the last time I lied like that to someone, Javier started to control my mind. And there was no *way* that I'd ever let that happen again. With all these demons and thoughts racing through my head, I needed to stay in control this time, because now I had to worry about Dr. U, Trevon, the red-eyed woman, and a looming war with angels.

Instead of lying through my fangs, I smiled as sweetly as I could. "Don't worry about me right now. You need to recover before you even think about going back to work to fix someone else," I whispered, trailing my fingers across her cheeks and staring into her ocean blue eyes.

"You're not work, Dani. You're like my daughter."

My heart warmed at her kind words, my eyes filling with tears. While Dr. U had raised me and had been there through everything with me, I didn't think that she thought of me as a daughter, just like I thought of her as a mother. Most days, especially when I was younger, I felt like a nuisance. All I did was sit in her house, cry my eyes out, and wake up screaming in the middle of the night from demon-filled nightmares.

"Tell me," she continued.

Knowing that I couldn't even begin to speak about this feeling inside of me, I shook my head and reluctantly pulled my hand away from hers. "You need to get some rest. I will try my hardest to find you a doctor from Pride to come heal you. They're the best in all of Hell. For now, our doctors will look after you as best as they can."

Before I could step away, she grasped my hand in her weaker one and smiled. "Dani, you did great today. You're becoming stronger just like your mother and father must've been. I know that you probably don't think so, but I am so proud of you."

Unable to stop the grin on my face, I stared down at her with tears in my eyes as the warmth spread throughout my body. Even after everything that happened today, Dr. U was proud of *me*. I just hoped and prayed that she'd get better soon, so I could repay her for always being there for me.

A Lust doctor appeared at the door with piercing black eyes and ruffled hair. "Dr. Uriel," he said with a smile. "I've heard great things about you from Dani. I'm Dr. Cald, and I'll be taking care of you until you're strong and stable enough to move to the Pride hospitals to get treatment or until you're well enough to go through the portal to Earth again. It takes a lot of human energy to get from one side of the portal to the other, and if you're not prepared nor physically strong enough, you won't make it."

"How long will it take to heal her?" I asked.

He walked closer to her to examine her injuries and brushed his fingers against her bandages. "Down here—for a human—a long time. But Pride has some medication that will hopefully speed up the process, though I'm not positive that it'd work. You will have to talk to the Pride doctors."

As immense sorrow washed over me, Eros squeezed my

shoulder. Dr. Cald nodded to the other side of the room, just out of earshot from Dr. U. "Can I speak with you, Commander?" he asked, giving Dr. U his best smile that didn't quite reach his eyes.

After grabbing Eros's hand, I hurried with him to chat with Dr. Cald. "What is it?"

Dr. Cald pursed his lips together. "Her injuries are extensive. If you didn't stop it when you did, she would've been dead by now. I'll try everything that I can do, but there's no saying that she will survive this."

My heart sunk. "What?" I whispered.

"She has a few days in Lust itself at the very least, before it's vital to move her to Pride. Pride doctors are typically more well versed in demon injuries. We just mainly deal with…" He paused. "Sex related stuff, as you know. They should be able to help her extend her lifespan by a few more months or heal her completely, based on the science and magic that they know over there."

"So, I should worry," I stated, making it clear. My insides tightened at the thought of losing Dr. U, my anxiety spiking so high that, for a moment, I thought that Javier was back to control my mind for good.

"Don't worry until she gets to Pride. Right now, I must advise you to relax," he stated. "After what happened at the crowning ceremony, you need to cool off, keep your heart rate down, and try to find some peace. Those demons' souls won't stay quiet for long."

Nodding my head, I turned back to Dr. U. Jasmine glanced over at me and gave me the weakest of smiles. "Go, and do what you need to do. I'll stay with her," Jasmine offered quietly from the corner of the room.

I glanced over at her, yet she looked back at the window almost instantly—still unable to hold eye contact. I gave her a curt nod, kissed Dr. U on the forehead, and walked out of the room with Eros, vowing that I wouldn't relax fully until I found my doctor from Pride to heal my mentor.

Once we departed from the spare room, Eros grabbed my hand, his grip tight, almost as if he was not willing to let me go, like he wanted to hold me close forever and ever. We walked down the high-ceiling halls to my office. Inside, my desk was torn apart, books had been thrown, my bookcase toppled over, and pages from old and ancient books were scattered all over the floor.

Trevon's adventures as a demon last night certainly had consequences.

As soon as we walked in, Eros dropped my hand and shut the door. "We need to talk."

I sighed to myself, picked up a few books from the floor, and placed them onto the desk, fingers brushing against the hundreds of pages that weren't in my native tongue—but in a demonic language that I hadn't fully mastered yet but was learning slowly.

"What do you want to talk about?" I asked, leaning against what was left of my desk.

Eros lingered by the door, those devilish emerald eyes taking me in, almost in caution. My stomach tightened, more guilt washing over me at the sight of him. To see the caution and fear in his eyes hurt me.

Without saying anything, he walked toward me and stopped about a foot away. We were close, but not as close as we had been. I could tell that Eros was holding back, staying away in case something bad happened again.

"You're afraid of me," I whispered before he could say anything.

Instead of responding right away, he gently grasped my face and frowned. "Dani, I'm not afraid of you," he said, brushing his thumbs across my cheeks and stroking them gently. But Eros was lying.

"I can feel your fear," I whispered again, not knowing how I could sense it... but it was definitely there and only getting stronger by the moment. Eros had told me that those demons trapped in the portal could feel fear, that they preyed on it… And now I understood why.

It made a demon seem weak, but my Eros wasn't weak. He was vulnerable and hurting.

Eros glanced down between us, remorse washing all over his face. I grasped his jaw and shook my head. "Please, don't be afraid of me," I pleaded, tears threatening to fall. "You're my best friend. I can't do this without you. I need you to support me down here."

Because I kept unintentionally pushing people away. First, Kasey. Then, Jasmine.

A few months ago I hadn't even known that Hell was a thing, and now I was the queen of one of the most powerful kingdoms. If I needed anyone at this time, it was Eros right now. He had been the Prince of Lust for thousands of years; he knew how this kind of thing worked.

"Are you still… hungry?" he asked carefully.

After I shook my head, Eros blew out a deep breath, wrapped his arms around my waist, and slumped his head down so it was resting in the crook of my neck, all the muscles in his body relaxed the way they did after sex. "Hell, Dani, I thought you lost control completely. I thought I'd never see you, sane and calm like this, again."

I wrapped my arms around his shoulders and tugged him closer to me, burying my face into his neck. "This is me. The Dani you fell in love with. You don't have to worry. I promise that I'll never do anything to hurt you."

We held each other in silence for a few moments, his scent of cinnamon calming my senses. "That was the first time you devoured that much," Eros finally said. "Your appetite for demon souls will continue to grow. It will become harder and harder for you to control your urges when you're not satisfied."

"Which means that I'll need to be satisfied, right?" I joked, awkwardly hoping to lighten the mood. I poked him in the stomach, feeling his hard abdomen underneath his shirt, and smiled up at him. "You're good at doing that."

Eros hesitated. "Maybe, but not for long. Without more sex, you're going to crave more souls. It's one or the other, Dani. I'll provide you with as much as I can, but I won't be enough. You're Queen of Lust now. Your demon will require more of everything."

I pressed my lips together, not wanting to have this conversation with him again. I wanted Eros and only Eros, having someone else in this relationship with us was enticing but it was also so terrifying at the same time. I trusted him with everything that I had… but it could lead to drama, and Lord knew that I didn't need more of that in my life.

"I don't want to," I whispered.

"You don't want to, but it needs to be done."

"Well, what do you suggest?" I asked, trying to compromise. "I want you to be happy with this decision, whatever it may be. There are a lot of demons in Lust who'd want to be with us, just because we're the commanders. And I want someone who will love us for us, not because of our title."

"You're the commander," he clarified. "Not me."

"We're in this together. I can't run an entire kingdom by myself. I need you to trust me, and I need to be able to trust that whatever decision we make isn't going to cause you stress. The beginning of the end is here. Demons will rise soon. I'm only strong with you by my side."

A deafening silence captured the room, then Eros swallowed. "What about Lucifer?"

"Lucifer?" I asked, brows furrowed together.

It shouldn't have surprised me, as Lucifer was growing closer to both of us and Eros had mentioned it before. But Lucifer had an entire kingdom to run himself, he couldn't be in my bed every night, could he?

"Lucifer isn't going to use either of us for power or control, since he already has a kingdom of his own. He likes spending time over in Lust, and don't you enjoy our little trips to Pride?" Eros asked.

I hesitated but nodded. "Is this what you want? Are you okay with me being with one of your greatest friends all the time?"

Eros paused again, taking a long time to answer my simple question and I could tell that there was so much he wanted to say to me, but instead he opted for a simple: "Yes, I want you healthy and in control of your urges."

"Is this what *you* want?" I repeated, wanting him to come out and say it. "Do you want Lucifer to be with me and with *us*? Adding someone else to this mix, even if it's just for casual sex, might get a bit messy. One of us could end up *catching feelings.*"

Because I wasn't going to lie, Lucifer was easy to fall for.

"Us…" he repeated with a smile, grabbing my hands. "I'd like for him to join us."

What seemed like ages ago now, Eros mentioned that he only liked sex with people he had feelings for, and while Eros and Lucifer hadn't had sex with each other—at least to my knowledge —Eros had kissed Lucifer the other day and enjoyed it too.

Maybe he did want this more than I thought.

"Let's talk to him and not settle until we are certain that this is something he desires."

Eros grasped my jaw, pulled me toward him, and kissed me. "Good," he mumbled against my lips. He wrapped his arms around the back of my thighs, picked me off the floor, and placed me on the desk. "Because I want to be able to enjoy my time with you now, Dani."

I drew my finger up the side of Eros's neck and under his chin, forcing him to look at me with those sinful emerald eyes that I wanted to consume every night until the end of time. He hardened against the front of his pants, grinding himself into me softly.

"Are you afraid of what will happen to me when you thrust yourself inside me, Eros?" I murmured against his lips, letting myself have just a taste. "Are you afraid that I'm going to lose control and devour every bit of you?" I inhaled his cinnamon scent deeply and shuddered in delight. "Or are *you* afraid that you're going to love it too damn much?"

Eros wrapped a hand around my neck and pushed me back with it, his claws dangerously close to my throat, strumming his fingers up and down. I sucked in a breath, feeling the heat gather in my core and spread throughout my body.

When he rested his forehead on mine and kissed me, I closed my eyes. We were suddenly transported to that realm that was both imagination yet truth, dream yet reality, the hazy in-between where all your dreams came true and all those monsters in your nightmares were real.

Instead of being in my old bedroom or any of the other places Eros mind-controlled me before, we were walking on white feathery clouds behind enormous golden gates, staring at miles upon miles of red apple trees.

Eros looked almost surprised that we ended up here, yet he grasped my hand and pulled from the path to behind some trees to hide as people with huge wings that I didn't recognize walked from a large temple down the path, all chatting quietly with each other.

He placed a hand over my mouth, pushed me against the tree, and grinded his hips against mine, emerald green eyes filling with complete darkness. Lust shot through my body at the thought of this being… so sinful that even Eros thought he had to hide. Eros never hid from anyone and took me where he pleased, like on the bus that one night.

While he played with my clit with one hand—teasing it in torturous circles—he pulled out his cock with the other, lifted one of my legs into the air, and pushed himself into me without hesitation. As soon as he filled me, my entire body shuddered in delight.

"You're going to scream for me, Dani," Eros said, staring down at me with black eyes. He pumped in and out of me as people walked through the path, not seeing us *yet*. "And when you do, you're going to be as loud as you fucking can. Do you understand me?"

My core tightened even more on him, and I nodded, sucking my lip between my teeth and holding my breath as the pressure rose higher and higher in my core. It had barely been a few moments, but I was already about to tip over the edge.

I guess that's what happened when I was already drunk off souls from tens of demons.

He stopped moving his fingers for a moment, the pressure subsiding slightly, then slapped his palm against the sensitive bud. I yelped out into his palm and grasped onto his shoulders, clawing at the muscle. Oh god, I was going to...

"Come for me, Dani."

Throwing my head back, I reached behind me, grasping at the tree trunk, at the leaves, at the apples even, anything that I could to hold me steady because my entire body was trembling in pure ecstasy. Wave after wave of pleasure rolled through me, and I let out a scream that came from so deep inside me I almost didn't recognize it as mine.

Eros continued to pump inside of me, filling me with more and more of his cum with every thrust. I clenched on his cock, wanting to suck the juices right out of it. He slowed down slightly, smirking against my neck and letting his teeth dip into my skin. "Heavens, Dani..."

Almost as quickly as they appeared, the feathery white clouds disappeared around us, and we were back in my office with his head buried in the crook of my neck. I took a deep breath, my chest rising and falling. "Where-where were we?"

Eros opened his hazy emerald eyes and pulled away, lips parted. "Heaven."

"Why'd you bring me there, out of all places?"

"I didn't," he said. "You brought us there."

CHAPTER 3

After my personal Queen of Lust celebration in my office with Eros, we decided to head to Pride to check up on Trevon and to talk to the doctor about helping Dr. U. Yet while we walked to the portal, hand in hand, all I could think about was the weird power I must've just unlocked.

Now, not only was I able to bring Eros to places during sex and put thoughts into his mind, but I brought us to Heaven. *Heaven*: a place that I had never, ever been to before. How'd I know what it had looked like with those clouds, golden gates, and apple trees? Was there more to Heaven that just that? Would I ever really get a chance to make it there?

Guards opened the gates to the busy portal room, where demons hurried to depart from Lust as quickly as possible. When people saw me, they parted a path in fear and allowed Eros and me to go through the portal first. I curled my hand around Eros's bicep and stepped into the black mist, expecting the wandering souls to claw at my legs and jagged teeth to pierce into my flesh like usual.

But even they stayed away from me, as if *they* knew about what happened too.

Approaching the exit for Pride, I glanced around at the hunting black eyes of demons watching me from the shadows. It felt unusual and uneasy to have even the darkest of souls be afraid of me. But when I stepped out of the portal and into Pride, they disappeared and coldness folded around me.

All the guards stepped away from me and toward the wall, holding their breath. Eros grabbed my hands and pulled me out of the portal room, leaving the black misty interior behind. Snow pounded down around us and melted almost immediately on the stone walkway, barely even leaving a bead of water in its wake. Bare trees rustled, their heavy branches scraping.

I made a beeline for the doctors' offices and briefly glanced over at the ashy-gray skies hovering over the Chains. Guards dressed in heavy ice armor stood around the building, scouting for potential criminal demons helping their friends escape.

Eros stopped and pursed his lips together, staring at the large prison that I locked Kasey in last night. She had told the truth about Maeve, and I felt bad for throwing her in there, but part of me wanted her to rot for a bit longer because of everything that had happened these past few weeks. She had been a total bitch to me. And while she might've been honest, she ruined my party, she refused to talk to me, and even tried to tear me down.

My own best friend did that to me when I needed her the absolute most.

Maybe I was too hard on her, but I was Queen of Lust now. I couldn't let Envies walk all over me anymore, especially not the one whose mother killed my father so she could become queen of a kingdom. I had to choose my friends sparingly now.

"Will you be okay talking to the doctor about Trevon and Dr. U yourself?" Eros asked me, awkwardly scratching the back of his head. Brown strands of hair blew into his tan face, snow melting against his forehead. "I need to talk to Kasey."

"Are you going to let her out?" I asked.

"No, I just want to talk."

After a moment of hesitation, I nodded. "You don't have to ask if it's okay. She's your sister."

When Eros paused, I gave him my best reassuring smile. Though Kasey and I weren't on good terms, I wasn't going to stop him from seeing her. From spending thousands of years in Hell, Eros was smart, wise, and understood how demons worked way more than I did. If he thought that talking to Kasey was a good idea, I wasn't going to stop him. He always had my back.

Once I urged him toward the Chains, I continued on the path toward the doctors' offices. I shielded my eyes from the blazing white sun reflecting against the snow and stared up at Lucifer's castle perched less than a mile from the doctor's, large ice-white clouds sitting somberly overhead.

Lucifer lounged on his balcony at least ten stories in the air with a glass of Vemon in his hand. He tilted his drink toward me, and I smiled back, Eros's words from earlier still sound in my head. Sooner or later, I would need someone else and Eros wanted that someone to be Lucifer.

"Come to chat?" Lucifer shouted, the wind catching his voice.

"Later," I called, disappearing around the building to the front.

A big blue sign that read *Closed for the Ceremony in Lust* hung on the doors. My stomach tightened, and I grabbed the handle anyway because I needed to see Trevon at least, but it was locked. I gnawed on the inside of my lip, found a side-door that hadn't been chained closed, and weaseled my way into the office, knowing that they had to be in here.

There was no way Trevon was able to recover that quickly. It took him weeks to recover last time.

Yet the office and the halls were completely empty, all the lights turned off and the silence overwhelming. I hurried to the back office, where I left Trevon in the doctor's care. Instead of barging in like I did last time, I knocked and waited patiently for him to answer it.

One moment passed. Then two. Then I started to fear the worst.

I banged again with the side of my fist, only left to be standing in front of a closed door for five more agonizing minutes. When nerves and frustration got the best of me, I kicked the door open and found the room vacant, just like the rest of the hospital.

Blood covered the table, papers laid across the room in a disheveled mess, and books had toppled over. I shook my head, my chest tightening and nothing but terror rushing through my thoughts.

Something happened. Something damn bad must've happened.

"Trevon!" I yelled, running through the office halls and thrusting open all the doors.

Where the hell was that man? And where had the doctor gone? It wasn't like I left them alone for days without any communication, but I had left them alone for *mere hours*, and now they were both gone.

After hurrying back to the back office, I eyed Trevon's blood and growled. Though I couldn't find any more traces of it throughout the hospital, it reminded me of the one and only red-eyed woman. If she had anything to do with this, I would be devastated that I hadn't taken care of her beforehand.

Maybe she wanted my head, now that I was Queen, and was taunting me by capturing and killing my ex-boyfriend and the greatest doctor in all of Hell. Maybe preparing for this war with Mother should be put on the back burner, so I could protect all the people that I cared about before then.

Whatever the damn reason that Trevon was gone, I would find him. I had to.

CHAPTER 4

Slamming the doctor's office door closed, I ran out into the blizzard outside and shielded my face from the searing cold snow. I pulled out my buzzing phone and placed it against my ear, hoping that whoever the hell was calling me knew about Trevon's whereabouts, because I couldn't let him tear up Hell as an angel or even let any demon in Hell figure out that he was a holy creature. They would destroy him within seconds.

"Hello?" I asked, getting a mouthful of snow.

"Dani," Maria said on the other end, voice soft and urgent.

I sighed through my nose, both relieved to hear her voice and stressed the fuck out that Trevon was still out there. Everything had been so loud in my mind today, but listening to her voice and knowing that she was okay when everything burned around me made me relax a bit.

"Trevon is at our apartment with this… *demon* guy who claims to know you," Maria said, pausing. She sucked in a breath, the sound of shuffling drifting through the phone. "Please, get down here. You know how much I can't really do the whole demon thing. He's freaking me out."

"Fuck," I whispered to myself, slapping a plam against my

forehead. Out of all the places Trevon could've gone, why was he there? Was he holding the doctor hostage or something? Did the doctor bring him there for a reason? And where the hell was Zane when Maria needed him?

"Why is he there? I left them both in Pride."

"The demon said that his skin was burning in hell, so he brought him here. He's apparently part angel?" Maria said, blowing out a deep breath. "Listen, I don't know how the *hell* Trevon could be half-angel, but, please, tell me that you're on your way."

"I'll be there as soon as I can," I said. After slipping my phone into my pocket, I hurried toward the portal.

Of course, Trevon's skin was burning and his angel was suffering. I just didn't think it'd have such an effect on him until after a day or so. It didn't have much of an effect at all, but I also had demon blood rushing through my veins.

Before I slipped into the portal room, I glanced over at the Chains surrounded by a thickening layer of gray clouds. I should've told Eros that I was leaving for Maria's, but Maria needed me now, I didn't want to see Kasey, and I needed to get to Trevon as quickly as possible.

After walking through the black mist and pushing demons out of the way through the darkness, I hopped out of one of the many portals on Earth near the Lounge. Streets crowded with confetti, beer bottles littering the ground, and hung-over men and women staggering home, the city was covered in a layer of snow and debris from the New Year celebration.

I made a beeline for the apartment and knocked not-so-patiently on the door, tapping my foot on the ground and wondering if I should just barge into the room and give that doctor a piece of my mind. Bringing Trevon here was *not* the smart thing to do. This apartment building was infested with demons.

Zane opened the door, smiling when he saw me. "Dani..."

"What's going on?" I asked, ignoring those lust filled eyes he was giving me and stepping into the room to smell... something roasting. "And where have you been? Maria called me basically crying because she was so nervous about the Pride doctor being here."

"Recovering from the Crowning Ceremony celebration."

"There was no celebration. It turned into a madhouse."

"*You* turned it into a madhouse," Zane said, guiding me to the living room, his scent filling my nostrils and awakening the demon inside of me.

After vowing to myself that I wouldn't let him get to me, I walked into the living room and stopped dead in my tracks, my chest tightening at the sight of my ex-boyfriend. Trevon laid on the leather couch with his eyes closed, red and blotchy burns all over his slightly bubbling skin.

"Holy hell, what happened to him?" I asked, rushing over and doubling over beside him.

Maria stood in the corner, keeping her distance from the doctor and gnawing on the inside of her cheek. There were tears in her eyes, and she shuddered when the sound of sizzling flesh drifted through the quiet room. "He's bad, isn't he?"

Glancing at the doctor, I shook my head. "How did he get this way? When I left him, he wasn't like this. Did you run any test on him? Take any blood? Do something to ignite this... this fire inside of him?"

The doctor looked at me with icy blue eyes and shook his head. "No. At the time of your crowning ceremony, his skin started to burn because of his angelic side. Your orders were not to test him, so I didn't touch him. Instead I brought him here, knowing that he'd be safe."

"Safe?" I snapped through my fangs, Javier's innate rage boiling inside of me. "This is probably the least safe place to be in all of Earth! It's infested with demons, and Sathanus knows where this place is." I grasped Trevon's hand and felt his skin ooze against mine. "You know that it's so much harder to distinguish angels from demons here on Earth."

At least down in Hell, I knew where he was and knew how to hide him. But being on Earth, especially during the time of the crowning, was not a smart idea, because I had no idea where he was and hadn't been informed that the doctor wanted to move him.

"It was that or he'd die in Hell. Angels alone can't survive down there."

"He survived down there while he was at the Chains," I said.

Playing with the tip of his horn of ice, the doctor nodded. "He was less susceptible to demons back then. Now he's been possessed twice. They will smell him out down there, know he's an easy target, corrupt him, and tear him apart from the inside out. Was that what I should've let happen, Commander?"

After glancing back down at Trevon, I shook my head and frowned. "No, but next time, I'd like to be informed before you make any haste decisions. Trevon is one of my greatest friends." I stood up and stalked over to the doctor, narrowing my gaze. "If he would've died in your care here, it would've been your fault."

I wanted to make that clear.

Trevon had been down in Hell because I invited him to that stupid party, thinking that everything would be fine because I was *watching* him. And I was slowly learning that demons were ruthless creatures that would do anything for a laugh. Lucifer said that I could trust this doctor, but I didn't know his true intentions, especially when he didn't contact me about him.

"How will you treat him here?" I asked the doctor.

"I don't have a direct answer for you at the moment. Angels who end up in Hell are never treated for their burns, so I don't know what will work. Though I have a couple ideas that I'll try as soon as I can head back down to Pride to retrieve medication and lotion."

Zane stepped forward and cleared his throat. "We know that

you have a lot going on, Dani, since you just became queen," Zane said to me and the doctor while glancing at Maria. "I can watch him here to make sure nothing happens to him while we find a cure."

I glanced back down at Trevon, brushed my fingers over his scorching forehead, and frowned. The burns didn't seem to stop and his skin just became redder by the second. Hesitantly, I raised my gaze again. "You will be able to find a cure, correct? You're not going to screw me over? Lucifer recommended you to me. You won't betray me and let him down, right?"

It came out as a slight threat, just as I needed it to be.

"I believe so. I have some medication that I gave him earlier, which slows the burning but it's just temporary. I need to run some tests and find something more sustainable," he said to me. "But I'll try my hardest to get it back up here as soon as possible."

"Hurry, because I need your help healing someone else as well."

"Commander Dani." The doctor grimmaced. "There are so many patients that I have to see in Pride. I don't know if I'll have time, and I cannot do anything else like this, keeping another angel under my watch. It is dangerous to even be here, especially with all the demons I see in my office. Someone will smell an angel out quickly."

Ushering him into the other room to relieve some of Maria's anxiety, I stopped by the floor-length windows and looked out into the snowy city landscape. "This doesn't have to do with another angel." At least, I hoped it didn't. "My therapist has been beaten and abused badly by two demons from Envy. She's a human. I want her to recover quickly, so she can get back to her normal life, and I need one of the Pride doctors to run some tests to make sure those Envies didn't give her any drugs from Hell."

"I'll see what I can do."

After he departed, Maria peaked his head into the room. "He's finally gone?" She glanced around just to make sure, rushed into the room, and threw her arms around me. "Zane told me what happened to you," she said, shaking her head and burying her face into the crook of my neck. "I'm so glad that you're okay. Those demons deserved everything that happened to them."

I wrapped my arm around her and walked back out into the living room, glancing down at Trevon who had fallen into a deep and agonizing sleep. With the burns still prevalent on his arms, I hoped that him being on Earth would help him, even just a bit.

"What exactly did he tell you about me?" I asked, arching a brow.

The microwave beeped, and Maria pulled away. "Hold on." She disappeared into the kitchen, and I narrowed my eyes at Zane. "What did you say to her about what happened?"

He sat down on the couch opposite to Trevon and leaned his forearms onto his knees. "That vicious demons had challenged you for your rightful spot." He cracked one of the typically, sinful smiles from Lust, dark hair falling into his face. "And that you used everything you had to defeat them. She doesn't need to know how you did it, how that angelic part of you turned bad, sucked out the souls of any demon who got in your way. What happens in Hell, stays in Hell, Commander."

I glided my tongue across the tips of my fangs. "Are you flirting with me, Zane?"

It was common practice amongst Lusts, but it also awakened that part of me I was trying to suppress at the moment. Losing control like that was only for Hell. It couldn't be brought to Earth. Who knew what would happen here?

The pupils in Zane's eyes dilated, almost capturing his whole eyes. But when he inhaled Maria's scent, they immediately returned to his normal human color, and he relaxed against the leather couch and looked over at the door.

"I made hot chocolate!" Maria said, walking back into the room with two steaming coffee mugs and handing me one. She sat down across from me and looked at Zane. "Do you want a cup too?"

Zane stood and shoved his hands into his pockets. "Nah, I'm going to grab some stuff from my place next door, so I can come watch Trevon tonight. I guess we're officially living together now, Maria. It's going to be a good time."

When Zane shut our apartment door, Maria turned to me with a grin. "Okay, I know how I always complain about demons and how they freak me out, but I'm so excited for Zane to be here. We've been on and off for the last couple weeks, but…" She jumped up and down in her seat, her hot chocolate nearly sploshing over the edge of her mug. "He's amazing!"

"In bed," I clarified with a smile.

She playfully smacked my arm, cheeks flushing red. "Don't have to say it out loud! He might hear you."

"He already knows it, Maria. All Lusts do."

~

Two hours later, I stomped the snow off my boots and walked into the Lounge, my gaze immediately finding Eros and Lucifer sitting at our usual table and smiling at each other. Even from afar, I could not only see the lust in Eros's eyes but the desire for Lucifer on the most intimate of levels. And while I wanted to feel jealous, I didn't, at all.

Maybe Eros was right, being jealous just wasn't in a Lust's nature.

But that didn't stop the Envies inside my head from making me think the worst. I pushed them away, deciding not to listen to them, because the last time I listened to a demon in my mind I almost killed the man I cared about the most.

Not Javier nor any other demon would make me that weak again.

When I walked to our table and slid into the red booth, Eros glanced up at me with his big sparkling emerald eyes and kissed me. "You made it in one piece," he said, tucking some hair behind my ear. "I thought you went back to Lust. I couldn't find you."

Lucifer chuckled, strands of his long white hair falling into his face, illuminated by a flickering candle. "I don't think she's the one you have to worry about, Eros." He turned to me and nodded to Eros, smirking. "You know how many demons want to jump Eros's bones? You can't leave him in my kingdom alone, especially in the Chains."

"Very funny, Lucifer," I said, grabbing Eros's Passion Delight and taking a long gulp of it.

"Slow down." Eros took his drink from me. "We don't want another episode with you hyped up on Lust like earlier."

I narrowed my eyes at him. "Episode?"

"Let her have another," the annoying waiter who always seemed to bother us here said, setting down three more Passion Delights in front of all of us. "It's nice to see you, Commander. I heard your crowning went... well."

The souls of Wraths gathered in my mind, screaming and shouting at me to take this man's soul.

Kill him. Kill him now. He's been nothing but a nuisance to the entire kingdoms.

"Thank you. You may leave now," I said through gritted teeth. I didn't have time for his drama today and didn't want to lose control again, not after what happened between Dr. U and Trevon. I had too much other shit to worry about.

"Oh, but, darling—"

I snatched his tie in my hands, yanked him down to me, and showed him my fangs. "Leave, before I kill you too."

After tugging himself away from me, he nodded and scurried back to the bar. Heart pounding against my ribcage and pure adrenaline coursing through my body, I licked my lips and turned back to the table to find Eros hoarding all three Passion Delights on his side.

"I don't want a Passion Delight anyway," I said honestly, knowing that it would tip me over the edge again. I had to pace myself now. I couldn't get drunk off them for nothing because my beast had awoken.

Lucifer leaned back, tipping his glass of Vemon in my direction. "The ceremony *was* wonderful, Dani," he said, those icy eyes sending chills down my back, chills that I welcomed wholeheartedly because my heart was warm with wrath and it felt good.

"Dani and I have chatted," Eros said after a couple minutes, grasping my hand and resting it on the table. "And we agreed that Dani needs someone to help her sustain her sanity, so she doesn't have to use souls to feed her hunger."

A deafening silence overcame the table as Lucifer looked between us, then set his drink on the table, and intertwined his fingers like business people do right before closing a big deal. And… maybe that's what this was: business to secure our kingdom.

"You're asking me to fuck your woman anytime that she wants it, Eros?" Lucifer asked.

Why does he have to be so blunt about everything? Yet, I found myself clenching.

"Eros isn't putting you up to this, is he?" Lucifer asked, leaning forward this time. The candle flickered over the sharp facial structure, creating an almost godlike complexion. Lip curled into a soft smile, he said, "He does have a thing for me."

Eros pursed his lips together, nostrils flaring just a bit. Though his face was stone cold at Lucifer's comment, I saw that same little spark in his eyes that I had seen earlier. I gnawed on the inside of my lip, staring back and forth between them.

They had been friends for thousands of years. One day, I planned to find out the truth about what really happened between them. Whatever it was, it was big because… Eros looked pissed off that Lucifer let it slip out of the bag. But I wanted Eros to tell me on his own terms, so I didn't push it.

"No, Eros suggested it but he isn't putting me up to this." I rubbed my sweaty palms together and tried once again to silence those demons in my mind. "It's just going to get worse. Being both an angel and a demon, I can't just accept and ignore the souls and the voices in my mind. I need someone else to help."

Lucifer looked over at me—really looked, more than his typical passing glance—and nodded. "Of course, I would never pass up a chance to sleep with the new Queen of Lust whenever she's craving my cock."

CHAPTER 5

Lucifer kicked the Lust Room door open and collapsed on the large oak bed in the center of the room, kicking off his shoes and socks and tossing them onto the velvet armchair. Eros shut the door behind us, his hands curled around my waist. Chains, tattered black ropes, and all kinds of sex toys hung from hooks on the opposite wall.

Pressing his hard cock against my backside, Eros grabbed a fistful of my hair and tugged it back, drawing his nose up the side of my neck and laying a sloppy kiss just below my jaw. Lucifer cocked his finger in our direction and patted his lap where he wanted me to sit. I grabbed Eros's hand and walked over to Lucifer, straddling his waist and pulling Eros closer.

Once Lucifer rested his hands on my waist, he raised his hips and grinded him against me, Eros rubbing against my backside. "You feel how bad we want you?" Lucifer asked, curling a finger around a strand of my brown hair and tugging on it.

I let out a soft moan and tossed my head back against Eros's chest, staring up into his black eyes. Two pairs of hands ran up and down every part of my body, around my breasts, between my legs, in my hair. Eros leaned down and kissed my mouth, slowly unbuttoning my shirt and letting my breasts fall out.

Lucifer undid my bra and captured my nipple between his teeth, staring up at me with those icy blue eyes. I grabbed his horn, reached behind me and took Eros's too, and moaned, bucking my hips back and forth against them both.

"I've been imagining taking you in bed since the crowning ceremony," Lucifer said, sucking on my breast and tugging softly. He reached behind me and dragged his hand up Eros's taut abdomen, then pushed him away. "I know you've been waiting for it too. Relax. Take your clothes off."

Eros stumbled back a few feet, the scent of Passion Delight drifting out of his mouth. He undid the buttons on his shirt, letting it hang on his muscular shoulders, and watched us intently. My pussy tightened, and I leaned into Lucifer to give him more of me as he laid back on the bed.

Dipping a hand between my legs and dragging his fingers up my thigh to my panties, Lucifer chuckled coldly against my ear. "Someone's excited for this." He pulled back on my horn and kissed up my neck. "Your panties are soaked through, Dani."

I whimpered, my core tightening. Eros crawled up behind me, sucking on the other side of my neck, and slipped his fingers underneath the waistband of my underwear and peeled apart my folds. "Dani," he murmured, blowing out a deep breath and glancing over my shoulder at Lucifer. "Wet enough to slide right into her."

Eros rubbed his cock against my backside, shoved himself into my pussy, and grabbed my hips. "Stroke his cock," Eros ordered into my ear, holding me up by a fistful of my hair. "Can you do that for me, Dani?"

Pussy tightening around him, I reached down and stroked Lucifer through his pants. Lucifer captured my nipples between his fingers and tugged on them harder and harder the faster I stroked him. Eros spit on two fingers, spread my cheeks, and pressed them against my ass.

Once I pulled off Lucifer's pants, I crawled closer to position him at my entrance with Eros. "I was going to pull out of you, Dani," Eros said, gently gnawing on my earlobe and pushing himself deeper into me. "But I want you to feel two cocks buried deep in your pussy."

Lucifer pressed his head against my pussy and against Eros's cock, trying to shove himself into me. I dug my nails into Lucifer's chest, letting a moan escape my lips at the feel of them both pushing themselves inside of me, the pain being quickly replaced with pleasure.

With both of them inside me, I curled my toes and moaned again. Everything was so tight that I could feel every inch, ever vein, every pulse inside of me. I furrowed my brows together and whimpered as Lucifer bit down on my nipple and tugged on my other one.

They both started to thrust into me—slowly at first, then wildly and savagely like they had every other time before. "Fuck her harder," Eros growled at Lucifer, ramming into me and sucking on my neck from behind. He slipped his fingers between my legs to rub my clit, driving me higher and higher.

Lucifer grasped both my breasts in his hands, as I bucked my hips back and forth to take them both. Wave after wave of pleasure rolled through my body, my legs trembling, and an unruly orgasm ripping through my body.

I threw my arms around Lucifer's shoulders, pressing my breasts against his chest and letting them both fuck me as hard as they wanted until they came inside of me.

~

"Are you coming back to Hell with us, Dani?" Lucifer asked after we walked out of the Lounge and into the alleyway near, where the portal could be opened. Two large demons stood near the back of the building, using their magic to create a black mist against the red brick wall.

I squeezed Eros's hand. "I'm going to stay for a bit. I need some time to think."

"We need to talk about your vision when you get home." Eros tugged me in for a kiss and curled his fingers into my hips, his scent of cinnamon drifting heavily in the air between us. "No putting it off like you did last time."

"Promise." I wrapped my pinky finger around his, smiling as snowflakes melted in his dark brown hair. "And we need to talk about Trevon too."

"Trevon?" Eros asked, brows furrowed. After I gave him that *I really don't want to talk about it right now* look, he locked his pinky around mine and nodded. "We'll talk about him. But don't stay out too late. You're Queen now. You have duties."

After kissing me once more and making Lucifer roll his icy blue eyes, Eros disappeared through the back alley portal to Hell with Lucifer. I stuffed my hands into my pockets, sank further down in my coat, and walked down the slushy street.

A sheet of white clouds laid upon the sky, hovering over the city. Street lights blinked and flickered above me. I didn't have a specific place in mind to visit, but wanted to roam for a bit in my old familiar world. The one down below was too stressful to even think straight sometimes. It was nice to interact with humans who didn't quite believe in devils and angels and wandered around without a care in the world.

Once I passed Ollie's Diner, I stopped at the corner and glanced down Fourth Street where Mom was murdered. A car's tail lights reminded me of those raging red eyes of the woman who had slaughtered her in cold blood. Memories flashed through my mind of the hallowing days that followed, wondering when I'd see her again, if that killer was going to find me and kill me too, if I'd ever see her killer die by *my* hands.

A tear slid down my cheek, and I pushed it away. One day I would find her and torture her until I thought she had enough. I didn't care if I had to hurt her for millennia. She would receive what she dealt out to the world. And I knew just the place to start my hunt for her: Wrath.

Only Wraths had eyes as sanguine as hers.

Biast might know something. It was a long shot, but it'd be worth it.

I brushed my fingers across my family ring and suppressed the urge to scream for her to come find me here, for her to *try* to kill me in the street like she wanted to that day over two decades ago.

"You can't just stop in the middle of the sidewalk. People are trying to walk." A woman shoved past me, sending me nearly stumbling over in the snow. I cursed at her under my breath and decided to continue past Fourth street, the holiday music from the skating rink drifting down the roads.

I walked toward the music, finding a sense of serenity in it, and grabbed a hot chocolate from the stands Dr. U and I worked at a week ago, before my life turned upside down. Sitting down on a metal bench, I smiled at the families skating on the ice and wished that could be me.

Young children laughed with their parents on the ice. Teenage couples held hands and spun around in circles. Even some older couples shakily took the ice with each other. With the snow drifting down softly and the moon glinting above, everything seemed so peaceful here.

This place always felt so serene, angelic almost.

"Beautiful, isn't it?" A young, handsome man sat down beside me. Pale face, medium-length black hair parted right down the middle, and dark brown eyes, he looked over and gave me the softest of smiles, nothing but innocence on his face.

For some ungodly reason, the demons in my mind started to growl and claw at my insides, pleading at me to let them free, demanding that I kill the man sitting next to me while I had a chance. I closed my eyes, begging them to shut up for a moment, and forced myself to smile back at him.

"It is," I said, opening my eyes.

Something about being in this man's presence made me feel... guilty for what I had done this morning, for killing tens of demons, sucking their souls, letting them become part of me, and destroying any hope of living on their own again.

I sipped my hot chocolate, tearing my eyes away from his lovely brown ones and staring emptily back at the ice skaters. Maybe I didn't deserve to even wish that I had my old life back. By becoming Queen of Lust, I had hurt so many people—both innocent and not.

"Don't feel guilty about what happened, Dani. Everyone makes mistakes."

My eyes widened slightly, and I narrowed my eyes at him and sat up straight. How did this man know my name? Who was he? And how could he have known what I've done? He surely wasn't a demon, at least not with a serene smile like his.

"How do you know my name?" I whispered.

He leaned closer to me, eyes glimmering white. "Let's just say that you're popular up in Heaven."

CHAPTER 6

"You're from Heaven?" I asked, standing and taking a cautious step away from him.

Though I might've trusted him for the brief two minutes I knew him, I narrowed my eyes and felt a lot more hesitant now. There were far too many people who wanted to get close to me just to hurt me, and an angel showing up after I was crowned queen was too coincidental.

The angel stood beside me and smiled. "No need to worry."

Looking him up and down, I tried to determine if this man was deceiving me or not. Maeve had changed me to be better, stronger, and smarter. I didn't blindly trust anyone who claimed to be from Hell *or* from Heaven. For all I know, this man could've been a Wrath, because he didn't look like an angel at all with his muscular frame and brown eyes, almost a black color.

"What's your name?" I asked warily.

"Minseok."

After staring at him for a couple more moments, I turned my attention back to the skating rink and watched a father pick up his fallen four-year-old daughter off the ice. "Sorry, I don't believe it."

"If you want to ask Mother what my name is, be my guest," he said, lips curled up into a soft smile, then chuckled as if this was all meant to be one big joke. "You know, I'd prefer she name me something that lasted throughout the centuries like Fujio or Enji. Something cool, you know. But I got stuck with Minseok."

I cut my gaze to him. "You're really an angel?"

He nodded, eyes glowing even whiter. "You don't believe me?"

"No."

He stepped closer, and I moved back. "I want to show you who I am."

"You can show me from there," I said, staring him down and trying to intimidate him with my fangs and eyes that I could feel were being consumed with the darkness. While I might've been half-angel, I had never spoken to one like this before, except Mom, of course.

Why would one just appear out of nowhere?

When he looked deeply into my eyes, they were completely and utterly glowing white just as Trevon's were earlier. I gnawed on the inside of my lip, my chest tightening and my heart telling me to run now. Nothing good could come out of talking with an angel who knew me while I knew nothing about them. But something held me back. I had so many questions for that woman up above. *Mother*, they called her. And I wanted those questions answered now.

"What do you want?" I asked.

When Minseok's eyes returned to normal, he nodded to the sidewalk leading away from the ice skating rink. "There are too many humans and demons here," he said, starting toward the deserted road. "Let's chat elsewhere."

While I didn't want to go, I found myself following a few feet behind him. I clasped my hands behind my back and lengthened my claws in case I needed to use them at any point during this *chat.* No way was I going to stupidly go into this without being prepared.

"No need to prepare to kill me," he said without even looking back at me. He continued walking down the road a few steps ahead, the melted snow icing over around him. "I'm not here to fight you. I've been sent by *Mother* to negotiate the terms of your reign in Hell."

"The terms?" I asked with a laugh. "Last I heard, she doesn't control Hell. I can do as I please down there and am able to rule my people and my demons however I would like. I don't need any angel or any god telling me what I can and can't do."

"You're correct," Minseok said, nodding his head. Snow drifted down around us, making the air around him look like a frozen paradise. "But Mother knows that you have questions about your mother and... Trevon."

My whole body went tense when Minseok said his name. I lost control for a second, wrapped my hand around his throat, and thrust him against the side of a metal building. "If you touched him, I'll kill you right here and now."

"Relax, we haven't laid a hand on him yet." Minseok gently grasped my hand, fingers so soft against my skin—nothing like a demon's grasp. "Now if you could let go..."

I tightened my grip for a few moments, then pushed him away from me, letting out a ferocious growl. Something was wrong about this entire thing. How'd they know so much? Were they always watching what went on in Hell? Did they have an insider?

Minseok straightened himself out. "Trevon's an angel, isn't he?"

After pursing my lips together, I nodded.

"Covered in burns from Hell?" Minseok continued.

"Yes," I said, keeping my gaze on him and refusing to move another foot.

"His skin will continue to burn if he's not treated properly by a doctor who has dealt with angels before," Minseok said. "It will burn and it will burn and it will burn until it has seared off completely and there is nothing but bones and muscles left on his body."

My body stiffened. The thought of Trevon aching that badly made my heart hurt, but I didn't know if this guy was telling the truth. I didn't trust him, not now, not when he appeared at just the right time to magically make everything better. I could barely trust the people close to me; I definitely couldn't trust… him.

"You're lying," I said through gritted teeth, even though I knew it to be true.

"If you don't believe me, wait and see, but by that time it will be too late to save him."

"We have a cure in Hell. My doctor is working on it as we speak."

Minseok nodded as if he didn't believe me either, then returned to his too-good-to-be-true smile. "On a better note, Mother wants to negotiate. She is willing to bring Trevon up to Heaven to heal him from the poisonous Hell, if you agree to meet with her on her terms."

I blew a breath out of my nose, acting as if I didn't give a fuck about Trevon… but deep down, I did. Those burns were bad. In the two hours that I was at Maria's, Trevon kept getting worse and worse.

"I'm not meeting with her," I said, staying cautious. If the prophecy was true, then soon we'd be at war with the angels. I didn't need them tainting my mind with *their* venomous ways. "If *Mother* cared about me or my mother, she would've reached out sooner, not when I ascended to be Queen of Lust and am preparing to destroy every bit of her and all that *goodness* she claims to have. She doesn't care, Minseok, she's just using this as an excuse to talk to me."

Minseok sucked in a deep breath. "She said that you'd be difficult."

"She doesn't even know who I am," I said.

She had no idea how difficult I would be on her. Demons

might've referred to her as Mother and angels might've believed that she was truly their mother, but she wasn't even close to being mine. I didn't have to listen to her.

"If you change your mind and want to contact me again, you shall meet me here near the skating rink," Minseok said, taking a step backwards toward the skating rink. "She'll always be here for you, Dani. You just have to believe in her."

~

Minseok had gotten in my head and made me feel all sorts of ways about goodness and about peace. He had brought out my angel more than I thought he could. And when he had departed, I had an urge to call him back almost immediately, my questions needing answers.

But I restrained myself.

Instead of heading back to Lust or through the city some more, I walked through the portals to Pride again and stood outside the Chains with my stomach in knots. I didn't know what possessed me to come back here, but I needed to see Kasey.

I wanted peace with her so fucking bad. She was my best friend.

Guards pulled open two heavy stone doors and flickered the light on in the windowless room. Demons scurried back into their cages, shielding themselves from the brightness. When I took my first step into the building and the doors slammed behind me, demons rattled their cages and spat in my direction.

Nerves zipping through me, I walked down the corridor of cages. I hadn't stepped foot in here alone ever, and the thought of facing Kasey again terrified me more than it should've. I ached, desperately, for her approval. Since the first night I met her in the bathroom at some restaurant, I had looked up to her.

Demons growled and yelled, reaching between the bars to touch and try to taint my skin. But I ignored them, continued on, and only stopped when I reached the last cell. Kasey sat in it with her back against the bars and pity on her face, refusing to look up at me. "Are you here to chew me out too, like Eros did earlier? Because if you are, I'm not interested in it, Dani. I fucking understand what I did and I'm the one who has to live with it."

"I'm not here to scold you," I said, toying with the key in my pocket.

All I wanted to say was that I didn't want her to hate or envy me anymore, but I couldn't get the words out of my mouth. So, instead, I shoved the key into the lock, prayed that I was making the right decision, and opened her cell door.

I should've confided in Eros before I let her out, but Minseok had clouded my corrupt thinking. For me, at this moment, setting her free felt right. Kasey wasn't the one who tried to hurt me. She tried to warn me that Maeve was bad news, and I refused to listen to her. That was my fault, and I couldn't blame her for that.

The other things she did… shouldn't land her in the Chains forever.

Kasey shot to her feet and stared at me with wide green eyes. "You're letting me out?"

"I apologize for not listening to your warnings about Maeve, but you hadn't talked to me for days. You were giving me the cold shoulder. You left me when I needed you the most. I couldn't trust you, especially when you barged right into my party the way you did," I said, pain and heartbreak consuming me. "It hurt me so much, Kasey."

Kasey paused. "So, what are you saying? Why're you letting me out?"

After pausing for a long moment, I came to terms as to why I was really here. It wasn't because I was good or guilty. It was because I was a desperate fool who wanted everything to go back to normal. I thought that this was the way to Kasey's friendship again.

"At some point, I'd like to be friends again," I admitted.

It was stupid.

I knew it was as soon as the words left my mouth.

"And you don't deserve to be locked in here for eternity. You have a life, and I'm sure Aarav and Mycah are worried about you," I said quickly so I didn't sound desperate. I hated how I felt this way, but everyone who I cared about seemed to leave me at some point.

Dad.

Mom.

Trevon.

Kasey pressed her red lips together and looked down at the bloody concrete floor between us. "How could we ever be friends again?" she asked, looking up at me with those cold eyes I had gotten all too familiar with. "You're Queen of Lust, and I'm part Envy, just like my mother and just like Maeve—two people who have been killed because of you."

I stared at her and promised myself that I wouldn't let my eyes fill with tears at hearing Kasey speak such vile things. It was all true, but they were out to hurt me and Eros, maybe to kill us even. Was she angry that we protected ourselves? Would she have been angry if we were the ones who died, instead of them?

"They would've killed us," I said to her.

"That doesn't make it right."

"And what would?" I asked through gritted teeth. "Your parents killed mine, Kasey. They weren't good people like you think they are. Maeve beat up Dr. U, nearly killed her too. What would you do if Maeve had killed Mycah? Would you just let it happen?"

Kasey flared her nostrils. "Those are two different things."

"No, they're not."

"Believe what you fucking want, Dani."

A deafening silence consumed even the most rowdy demons in the prison, and I tore my gaze away from her. "Go," I said quietly. "Before I change my mind and keep you locked up in here for eternity."

Kasey looked at me for a long time, her eyes wavering slightly, then took off down the line of cells and disappeared out the two exit doors. I closed the cell and rested my forehead against the bars, not caring if it seared part of my skin off anymore.

It sucked to be the only one trying in a friendship that I wanted so desperately to work. Maybe I should give up totally on it. That way it'd be easier for me and for everyone around. But something kept drawing me to make peace with her, and I hated that part of me who craved it too.

CHAPTER 7

When I returned to Lust and found Eros cleaning my office, I pushed him down into my chair and curled up into his lap. Without even asking me any questions, he wrapped his arms around me and held me to his chest, gently stroking my brown hair and whispering into my ear.

I pushed a tear off my cheek, feeling like a complete idiot, and whimpered into him. I missed Kasey so freaking much. I wished we never fell apart because she was one of the people who made me so much stronger.

After fifteen minutes of crying, I lifted my gaze. "I let Kasey out of her cell."

Eros tensed but continued to stroke my hair. "You miss her, don't you?"

Afraid that if I opened my mouth, I'd let out an ugly sob, I nodded.

Picking me up and walking up the spiral stone staircase to our bedroom, he gently set me down in his lap and gazed out into the Lust's beautiful maroon night sky, the glimmering pink light glinting off his face. "I love Kasey too, but she's her mother's daughter. An Envy, and a good one at that."

"What if I made the wrong decision?" I asked, fingers curling into his chest. "I just… I wanted to… to be her friend again. Did I…" I lowered my voice until *I* could barely even hear myself. "Did I fuck up?"

Eros pressed his soft lips to my forehead. "No, you didn't fuck up."

"Eros, I—"

Gently, he grasped my jaw and forced me to look at him. "You didn't fuck up. Don't think like that, Dani. You can't let anyone get into your head. If this decision turns out being the worst one you've ever made, then we'll deal with it and punish her together. You're not in this alone, and you'll never be." He pushed away one of my tears with his thumb. "We'll worry about that when the time comes."

Shifting in his arms so I straddled his waist, I brushed my fingers against my family ring and swallowed. "You don't think she'll come to the castle and look for revenge, do you?"

"I have already spoken with the guards and have forbidden it. All Envies are required to be cleared by one of us, before they can enter, even if they're just in one of the Lust Rooms downstairs. But..." Eros paused and hardened his gaze. "She will still be free to roam in Lust and at the Lounge on Earth. So, be careful with her, Dani. You're the queen now and everyone is going to want something from you."

My gaze dropped to our red silk bedding, and I crawled off his lap and onto the mattress, pulling him down with me. Fingers trailing over his cheekbones, I furrowed my brows at him and frowned. I had so much more responsibility than any other twenty-three-year-old on Earth. I had a kingdom, a freaking kingdom in Hell to lead. I couldn't let Kasey get the best of me.

Eros grasped my hand and intertwined our fingers, his green eyes staring into mine. "Are you ready to talk about what happened this morning during our little *session* on your desk? Because we can't put it off much longer. This is a new power for you and… unusual that you'd bring us to a place you've never witnessed before."

I shook my head, because I wasn't ready. I didn't know what the hell it was, but I needed to get that *and* Minseok off my mind. Shit had gotten just a bit crazier after I left the Lounge and strolled around the city.

"While we're at it, we can also talk about the angel I met today," I hummed.

"Angel?" Eros asked, tensing and sitting up in the bed. He turned on our bedside lamp, the bright yellow light mixing with the pink moonlight and creating an orange hue on our bedside. "Who was it and where did you meet them?"

"He said that his name was Minseok," I told Eros, tugging off my shirt and pulling the silk red sheets over my body. "After I left the Lounge, I walked to the ice skating rink. He sat beside me and started talking to me like he had been watching me for a long time."

"Minseok," Eros repeated to himself, staring past me at my vanity mirror as if trying to remember something. After a few moments of silence, Eros shook his head. "I've never heard of him. He must be a relatively new angel. When I was in Heaven, I knew everyone."

I arched a brow. "Is new to you 4000 years old because, by the way he spoke, he seemed like he was *Mother's* favorite. He was talking about how she wanted him to come down here to talk to me and how she has a proposition for me and in exchange for listening she'd heal Trevon."

"All angels think they're Mother's favorite, but she's only ever had one true favorite." Eros paused and looked in the direction of Pride almost subconsciously. "Lucifer was her favorite. I don't think she'd have another one after he fell. She's realized her mistake in putting all her faith into one angel and watching him fall."

To suppress the urge to laugh, I bit my lip and smiled. I could never picture Lucifer being God's favorite angel. Sure, she might've loved Lucifer but he definitely *couldn't* be the favorite. He was way too arrogant for his own good, and his pride… Did Mother inflate it too much?

"Anyway," Eros said, directing his attention back to me. "What'd he say to you?"

"He told me that Trevon wasn't going to get better down here where there is no one to help him, where the doctors—even from Hell—don't know how to heal an angel."

"What happened to Trevon?"

"His skin is burning. The doctor is working on a cure. The angels apparently can cure him, but I don't trust them one bit." I paused. "We should go over to Maria's tomorrow to see if Trevon is getting worse. I know that I shouldn't care about him after what he's done to me, but I don't want to see him die over this. Demons are cruel and have taken over his body one too many times. He can't handle it anymore."

"And you feel the need to protect him because he's part angel like you too?" Eros asked, in a tone that suggested he already knew it to be true. He took me in his arms again and smiled into the crook of my neck. "You know, that's what I love about you, Dani. You care."

My lips curled into a smile, and I playfully pushed him away. "Oh, don't get all cute on me. This is serious. They know me, know that I'm now a commander, and know about Trevon. It's terrifying to say the least, especially when we know nothing about them."

Eros rubbed my inner thigh. "They must've felt you thinking of them. It can happen, especially if you're dreaming of Heaven. They must sense that you want to keep peace or you feel guilty about what you've done. But…" He paused. "I don't want to stop you from going after a part of you that is there. Just because I left Heaven, doesn't mean that you have to ignore your angel or who you are or your feelings, but you must be careful. They act all holy and true, but they're suppressed."

I let out a laugh and shook my head. "I wasn't going to trust the man, anyway."

Though if I ever needed to, I could use him to my advantage. A couple times tonight, he got a bit too close to me, and I didn't miss the way his breath hitched when I shoved him up against that building. The way he looked at me was almost *sinful* for even an angel.

"Whatever you do, be careful," Eros warned.

"Always telling me to be careful of other people," I said, poking him in his hard abdomen. "But what about what's up here." I pointed to my head. "People should be afraid of me. *I* should be afraid of me. It's not right what I'm feeling, the souls festering inside me."

"You don't have anything to worry about as long as you feed." Eros placed his hands on my hips and pulled me closer. "So, about Heaven? Why did you bring me there?" he asked, drawing his thumb down my bottom lip. "Did you want to sin in the most devilish way possible, because I wouldn't mind doing that again..." He sucked in a sharp breath. "It brings back memories."

"Good ones?"

"Wicked ones."

~

I laid on the center yellow lines of Fourth Street and stared at the dark night sky above, cars and buses zipping by me, nearly running me over. Calming Christmas music played through the city from the ice skating rink, the sounds of children cheering and laughing making me relax for some odd reason.

Tilting my head to the left, I stared at Mom and me as a child, walking down the street with huge grins. Mom twirled me around, her favorite ice skates hanging off her shoulder, and laughed so angelically.

"You see her corruption?" the red-eyed woman said from above me, straddling my waist. "You see how a woman like her could never lead Hell with your father? That's why I killed her and that's why I will kill you one day too."

Those red eyes pierced through me, seemingly becoming the only thing I could focus on and brighter than the brightest twinkling star on the Christmas Tree I helped Mom put up the year she was brutally murdered. She lengthened a black talon and threateningly slid it across my throat. "Move, scream, or yell for your mother now, and you won't wake up."

Wanting to live to see another day, I pressed my lips together and stared at Mom and me. The red-eyed woman stood to her full height and zipped over to them. When Mom noticed her, she ushered little Dani along and told her to run to the ice skating rink and to never look back. And, stupidly, I ran.

I ached to run to the scene, to stop the woman from killing my mother, but I couldn't seem to move from the spot. I opened my mouth and no words came out.

When the red-eyed woman killed Mom dead, my throat closed, and I couldn't breathe. I grasped my neck, gasping for air and desperate to move, to breathe, to save Mom and to live. I couldn't live in this nightmare another moment. I couldn't see this nightmare again.

Four-year-old Dani turned around on the sidewalk and screamed through the night, the sound piercing, cutting, clawing through me. Dr. U sprinted out of the building to grab me, but this time the red-eyed woman murdered her too. I sat up, my legs heavy, and reached for mini-me. "Come here," I shouted to her, sanguine-colored tears streaming down my cheeks. "Come here, Dani!"

Almost as if time slowed down, Dani stared at me and sprinted through the traffic, jumping into my arms and burying her face into the crook of my neck. "Make it stop, Miss, please make it stop. I want my mommy back."

CHAPTER 8

With tears streaming down my cheeks, I sat up in bed and clutched the red silk sheets, an overwhelming sense of sorrow washing over me. To muffle my sobs, I placed a hand over my mouth and doubled over, praying that I would never have that kind of nightmare again.

Tying a purple silk robe around my waist, I kissed Eros on the forehead and left him to sleep while I snuck down the spiral staircase to Dr. U's floor. After watching her die in my dream… I couldn't ever even imagine it happening in real life. If someone killed her, they would be killing the final bit of hope left in me.

Pink moonlight flooded in through the large arch windows in the hallway and glinted against the marble floors. I took a deep breath, wiped away a couple tears, and opened Dr. U's door. Listening to her soothing and even breathing, I sighed and closed the door.

"Dr. U," I whispered more to myself than to her. I sat on the edge of her bed and frowned, the bruises on her face seemingly have gotten worse over the course of the last night. The doctor said that they would, but it hadn't looked like she made *any* improvement.

Instead of leaving and letting her rest, I climbed up onto the bed with her and curled into her like I used to do when I was a child. My fingers curled around her frail body, and I wept into her side—keeping my sobs as quiet as I could.

"Dani," Dr. U whispered, voice hoarse. "What's wrong?"

Tears streamed down my face, and I bit my lip hard enough to draw blood. "I love you so much, Dr. U," I whispered, clutching her tight but careful not to hurt her. "I know that I haven't told you much, but thank you for everything you've done for me. You've made me the woman I am today."

"Oh, Dani," she murmured, thumb brushing against mine. "That was all you."

"I'll do anything to make sure you heal as quickly as possible," I said, intertwining our fingers. "I'm not going to let you die down here. You deserve everything good in this lifetime."

After visiting Dr. U, I tied my purple silk robe tighter around my body and sauntered down the spiral stone stairs from Dr. U's room to the kitchen. Jasmine's sweet scent drifted through the house, tantalizing me in its wake. I tensed at the dreadful thought of confronting her this morning. I desperately needed to apologize for what I did, but apologizing was damn hard sometimes, especially to someone I hoped wouldn't leave me.

When I entered the kitchen, Jasmine was washing some dishes in the skink and didn't look over at me, though she tensed. I sat down at the table, which was already laid out with plates, glasses, Fervor Crisps, and French toast.

I picked up a fork and shoved it into a Fervor Crips, nervously glancing over at her. "Jasmine, can we talk?"

Jasmine shut off the sink and hurried over, wiping her wet hands on her white apron. "Is breakfast okay? Do you need some more Fervor Crisps for Eros?" she asked, avoiding the conversation just like I wanted to do too. She turned back around to hurry to the refrigerator. "I can get you some more tea."

Before she could walk away, I grasped her hand in mine. "No," I whispered, standing up to offer up my seat. "Sit down."

Jasmine hesitated for a few moments, then sat her petite body on my chair, anxiously running her hands through her hair. "Are you sure, Commander? I have so much to do. I really should be getting to it before Eros comes down."

"Have some breakfast," I said, pouring her some orange juice and placing some Fervor Crisps on a clean plate. I gave it to her and gnawed on the inside of my cheek, hoping that she'd accept it. "You've been working so hard lately."

Jasmine shook her head, still not making eye contact with me. "Command—"

"Dani," I corrected. "I told you to call me Dani."

She glanced up at me, her eyes softening a bit. "Dani," she said, my name rolling off her plump lips. "I really shouldn't be sitting around now. Eros hired me to make you both breakfast and clean around the palace. It's... it's fine. Really."

"Have some breakfast with me, please." I sat across from her. "We need to talk about what happened yesterday morning."

Jasmine reluctantly drank some of the orange juice, her gaze flickering to the silky robe around my torso. I pulled it together, scenting her arousal, and tied it tighter around my body because I couldn't get excited right now, not with her after what happened during the ceremony.

Once Jasmine started eating, I picked at a Fervor Crisp and watched her steadily. "Jasmine, I wanted to apologize for what happened at the ceremony. I never meant to lose control like that and nearly kill you. I understand if you want to leave this kingdom and never come back. If being around me makes you feel uncomfortable, you don't have to stay here. I have talked to the managers at the Lounge and your position is still available."

"Do you want me to leave?" she asked and grabbed my hand, almost in disbelief.

My eyes widened. "No, I don't want you to leave. But I wanted you to know that if *you* want to go, I won't have any hard feelings against you." I would be so fucking sad, but I wouldn't hold it against her. This was my fault. I let things get out of hand. I couldn't control the desire inside of me to consume more.

Before I pulled my hand away, Jasmine yanked me forward and pressed her lips right against mine, giving me a hot, heated, and much-needed kiss. I tensed for a moment, and when I realized that I wouldn't unintentionally suck her soul, I relaxed.

When she pulled away, she smiled at me. "I don't want to go."

I stared at her, my lips curling up. "You don't?" I whispered.

She shook her head. "I like being here with you."

My heart warmed, and I brushed my fingers against her cheek to draw her forward. I rested my forehead against hers, breathed in her scent, and slumped my shoulders forward. Though I hadn't known her for a long time, she had been one of the only ones to stay by my side no matter what and she had calmed me down greatly.

A few moments later, Eros walked into the kitchen. Jasmine quickly pulled away with flushed cheeks and smoothed out her apron, hurrying to make him a plate of breakfast. "Eros, sorry, I was—"

Eros grabbed an empty plate from her and smirked. "Don't let me interrupt you."

"You didn't interrupt anything. I was just... going to clean..."

"Dani's filthy mouth?" Eros asked, placing some Fervor Crisps on his plate and sitting across from me. Lips curled into a smirk, he sipped some orange juice and looked at me. "Did she do a good job?"

I rolled my eyes at his playfulness and shushed him because, though Jasmine was a Lust demon, she looked completely embarrassed right now. Jasmine undid her apron and hung it up near the pantry, padding across the marble floors.

"Jasmine," Eros called before she left the room. She turned around and peeked a glance at me. "Make sure you're around when we return to Hell tonight. Lucifer will be here, and I'm sure Dani will want some company."

My cheeks flamed, and I shot him mini-daggers from my eyes. Jasmine nodded and disappeared into one of the hallways, her scent still lingering in the enormous kitchen. Eros picked up a Fervor Crisp from his plate and nodded to the castle exit. "We have to go to see Maria. They called this morning while you were… *ahem*… flirting with our maid."

"I was *not* flirting," I said, stumbling on my own words. "I was apologizing."

"With your tongue?"

"Matter-of-fact, yes, with my tongue," I said.

After quickly dressing into something more acceptable for Earth, I hurried after him to the castle doors and out into Lust. Cherry blossoms rustled in a wind that seemed to have rolled over from Pride. I stepped closer to him as we walked down the white stone walkways and hugged my arms around my body.

"How's Dr. U doing? I heard that you went to visit her this morning," Eros said.

I gnawed on the inside of my lip. "Not good. And Trevon? What did Maria and Zane want? Is he getting worse?"

For a few moments, Eros didn't say anything. And as the moments went by, my heart shattered more and more. If Eros couldn't answer a simple question, Trevon must've been doing worse, and I didn't know if I'd be able to handle seeing him how he was.

Knowing that I could save him, if I asked the angels for help.

Knowing that all his pain could disappear at the snap of Mother's fingers.

Knowing that I would never be able to accept their help, because of pride and betrayal.

I curled my fingers around Eros's bicep, walked with him through the black misty portal in the velvet decorated portal room, and stepped onto Earth's concrete on the other end. The portal guards bowed their heads to us in respect, quickly closing up the alleyway portal before anyone saw.

Like it usually did in the city this time of year, it was snowing *again*. It was kind of pissing me off how cold it was here all the time, because I had gotten so used to Lust's mild temperatures. Traveling back and forth every day between frigid and warm made me want to pull my damn hair out.

After taking a shortcut to Maria's apartment, we knocked twice on the door. Not a moment later, Zane answered it with bags under his eyes and his hair in every direction as if he had been pulling it out. "Thank Satan that you're here. He's driving me crazy."

Taking Eros's hand, I hurried into the apartment and stopped dead in my tracks when I saw him. Trevon's usually dark brown skin was red, blotchy, and peeling. He sat up from the couch, his muscular back in scars and bubbling.

I walked over to him and held my breath, the disgusting scent of char drifting through my nostrils. I placed a hand on his thigh and rested my forehead against the side of his face, hoping that my touch would take away some of his pain. "You're not going to die, Trevon. We're finding someone to heal you as we speak. A doctor is coming." I looked up at Zane. "A doctor *is* coming, right?"

Trevon grabbed my hands. "I'm fine, Dani," he said, smiling. But even his best smile couldn't hide his thinning and reddening guns by his teeth or the pain I saw in his eyes every time he looked at me. Trevon definitely wasn't fine.

"You're not," I said, urging him to lie back down. "You need to rest."

When someone knocked on the door, I glanced over while gently rubbing Trevon's thigh. Pride's best doctor walked into the room with a bottle of medication and three tubes of some lotion. After he handed me one, I smoothed it against Trevon's burns, praying that this was helping, even in the slightest.

"Those are the last tubes that I have," the doctor said. "Please, make them last."

"What happened to the others?" I asked, brows furrowed together.

Maria held the small living room trash can up, showing me the two tubes inside. "He's gone through two since last night and keeps complaining about the pain. Is three going to be enough to last much longer?"

The doctor leaned over Trevon, placing his hand upon his head and grimacing. "I'm not sure. He's extremely warm, almost as hot as Wrath."

"Isn't there anything you could do? Anything at all? I need him to improve his health..." Because I did not want to ask Heaven for the help or the medication. God only knew what she'd do with him once she brought him up there.

I had heard too many horror stories from the people in Chastion and Eros about her.

"I have tried almost everything," the doctor said, shoving his hands into his pockets and cocking his horn toward me while he looked at Trevon. "If he doesn't start healing in a few days, I don't know if I can save him."

CHAPTER 9

With all the rumors floating around Hell about Heaven and Mother, I began to think that if Trevon had to go to Heaven, *Mother* would use him against me to get me to yield to her. I refused to bring him there, especially if she just wanted to use him as bait. But how could I let the man that I once loved, the man I had grown up with, just die for the sake of Hell?

I didn't want another death to weigh down on my shoulders.

Eros rubbed my shoulder slightly to calm me as we walked back to Lust through the black mystical portals. After the doctor told me that there wasn't much that he could do and that he didn't even know if a cure could exist, I had been struck with an overwhelming sense of anxiety.

Knowing that one of my best friends could die was almost worse than having Mom die suddenly. It gave me time to think, for the pain to fester, to blame myself for everything that had ever happened to him before this very moment.

Though Trevon had burned me one too many times, especially with sleeping with Javier, I didn't want him to die. He was part angel, just like I was, so I was hoping that *if* we had to bring him to Heaven, Mother would treat him with respect.

When the portal opened and we stepped into Lust, one of my guards bowed to me. "Lucifer is waiting for you at the castle," he said, holding out a platter of Passion Delights that every Lust received on their return to our kingdom.

Eros grasped my hand, gently stroked my knuckles with his thumb, and pulled me down the white stone walkway, which was littered with pink petals from the trees lining the sidewalks. I glanced up at them and followed their path as it led toward the garden of roses. I hadn't been back there for so long. I wanted to travel back in time to when I first came here, when Eros and I had a cute little picnic, before I had stolen so many demons' souls and didn't have these pestering voices inside me.

Instead of heading there though, Eros grabbed me and led me toward the castle where Lucifer stared out at the balcony from the bar area at us. He leaned over and smirked, his icy eyes making me shiver.

Even from two stories below him, I could smell the thick scent of his arousal as if he had been waiting a long time for us to come home from Earth. A wave of pleasure rolled through my body as I walked up the steps, my arm looped around Eros's arm, and pressed my thighs together.

Once we stepped it into the bar area, Jasmine had two drinks in her hands and gave one to Lucifer who now sat on some couches. We walked over to them, Eros's hand on my lower back and my heart racing fast at the thought of just relaxing tonight. God knew that I needed it more than anything right now.

Jasmine handed me a glass of Passion Delight and sat behind me on one of the bar sofas, her soft legs around my waist and her breasts grazing against my back. "Relax," she whispered, her hands gently massaging my shoulders.

I took a long sip of my drink and let myself relax in her arms, lying back against her. She moved her hands lower, looking over my shoulder and at my breasts as she brushed her fingers against my hardening nipples.

"I bet all that tension is just built up inside of you," Lucifer said from across the sofa. "All those souls just waiting to be silenced. They're talking to you, aren't they, Dani?" He cracked a smirk and trailed a hand up my leg, crawling closer to me. "What are they saying to that sinful mind of yours?" he asked, his icy-minty breath fanning my mouth. He slipped his hand between my legs and under my dress.

Unable to speak without whimpering, I pressed my lips together and spread my legs, letting him touch my wet panties. He chuckled and looked back at Eros. "She's so fucking wet tonight."

Jasmine continued to massage my breasts and, at one point, pushed the straps of my dress off my shoulders. I grabbed her hands, wanting to feel them on my skin, and pushed them under the cups of the dress so she could grasp my breasts.

I let out a breathy moan and arched my back, spreading my legs wider to give Lucifer better access. My gaze flickered to Eros, and I reached out for him to come closer. With a huge bulge in his pants, Eros walked over to me and knelt by the couch, fingers brushing against my lips. "What do you want, Dani?" he murmured against me.

My eyes fluttered closed at the light contact. "Lucifer to fuck me," I whispered. "Jasmine to rub my clit." I let out another moan as Lucifer pushed two long fingers inside of me. "You to kiss me."

Power swelled inside of me, and for a moment I thought I was going to lose all control again. My entire body tensed, and I squeezed my eyes closed. So much tension, so much… I opened my mouth and felt my entire body shake with pleasure as Lucifer curled his fingers inside of me. My chest heaved up and down as Jasmine tugged on my nipples. Tingles shot up and down my arms and legs. I moaned so loudly that my voice echoed through the entire palace.

Eros kissed me on the lips. "This is what happens when you learn to control yourself and those voices inside of you. You orgasm like this," he said. He slapped his hand over my clit, just one time, and I felt more pleasure rush through me.

Holy Hell. Holy fucking Hell.

My body trembled as Jasmine let out a breathy laugh in my ear. Wave after wave of ecstasy rolled through me, and I couldn't stop it, no matter how hard I tried. I could feed the demons in my head with more souls or I could decide to quiet them with this… pure delight.

Lucifer pulled his fingers out of me and undid his pants, pulling out his cock and positioning himself at my entrance. Jasmine trailed her fingers down my abdomen and to my clit. "Spit on it, Lucifer," she said to him.

Lucifer let spit drip off his lips and onto my pussy, making it glisten. She rubbed it around on my clit, getting me nice and wet and tense once more. As Lucifer pushed himself inside of me and Jasmine touched me just as I wanted, Eros pressed his lips to mine, stuck his tongue into my mouth, and gently caressed my nipples with his thumbs.

My body squirmed under Lucifer's as he pumped into me, his cock feeling so big inside my tight little hole. I let my body completely relax against Jasmine and turned my head to kiss her too. She smiled against me and rubbed my clit even harder.

"Are you going to come for us again?" she murmured against my lips.

I furrowed my brows together and nodded my head. "Yes."

Eros grasped one of my horns and pulled me toward him, pressing his lips to mine. "Come, Dani," he commanded. And, just like that, I came undone yet again, screaming out his name. But tonight was far from over. We were just getting started.

CHAPTER 10

Standing in the Garden of Roses and smelling the petals, I watched curiously as families of demons wailed around me. Some families were those from Wrath who had black flowers burning around them, others from Envy who picked and stole my beautiful lush roses, and even others were from Lust itself who embraced each other with pity.

Besides the horns and the devilish eyes, almost all the families looked like normal human ones, as if they cared about their young, their old, their mothers and fathers with everything they had. They weren't all bad like so many people thought.

I walked from group to group and saw the caracess of men and women I murdered at my crowning ceremony. When I walked to the Wraths, I felt their pain hidden behind their rage and fire. When I walked to the Envies, I felt their agony stowed away behind envious eyes. When I walked to the Lusts, I felt their hurt through every one of their emotions.

So many families had been torn apart because of me.

Suddenly all those people turned in my direction and started at me in a frightening manner. My powers felt so weak that I couldn't even use them. I backed away slowly, but my legs wouldn't move that quickly. Instead, I stumbled back onto my palms and ass, scurrying away through the beds of roses.

Yet they kept coming and coming and coming until they had surrounded me completely. Their hands all over my skin, their teeth sliding into my flesh, their claws tearing me apart until I could barely breathe. I felt like I was suffocating in the sea of demons surrounding me.

I reached my hand up, needing fresh air. Someone grabbed my arm and pulled me out of the group of people and onto Earth. Minseok stood there smiling at me and rocking back on his heels. "How about that help now, Dani? Do you need our help? Tell me your sins and you'll be cleansed of them."

Pulling my hand out of his, I stared behind him at Mom, or the ghost of her. She shook her head at me, mouthing at me not to trust him with tears welling up in her eyes. She reached out for me and then the red-eyed woman slashed her claws through her neck and she fell.

I screamed and ran over to her body. But, when I made it there, she had disappeared and Minseok stood in her place, asking me if I needed his help, telling me that I needed his help to defeat the darkness inside of me. It would just build higher and higher if I didn't try to stop it now.

I glanced behind him again to see Mom shaking her head and mouthing at me not to trust him. The red-eyed woman killed her again, and the same process repeated over and over again until one time the red-eyed woman looked right at me.

"You're next," she cackled, smirking at me with red in her eyes.

Tears streamed down my cheeks. "I'll kill you first," I said.

"You'll kill me only when everyone else that you love is dead, and all their souls are in your body," she said to me, licking my mother's blood off her fingers. "You don't have control of your powers. You never will."

Then she sprinted right at me and suddenly I was back in the swarm of bodies of demons I had hurt. They held me down, kept me in place, as the red-eyed woman thrust her claws into my neck and killed me dead.

I screamed at the top of my lungs, sat up in the bed, and clutched my neck, gasping for a breath. Air filled my lungs, yet, still, I felt like I couldn't breathe. I grasped my neck harder, still feeling the claws plunged into my throat and tried to pull them out even though they weren't really there.

"Dani," Jasmine said from beside me, sitting up in the bed and rubbing my shoulders. She pulled the blanket over her bare chest and desperately tried to pull my hand away from my neck. "Stop it. You're choking yourself."

But I still couldn't breathe. The guilt of killing people from all those families, the hurt of Mom, those red eyes were all weighing heavily on my shoulders and crushing me from the inside out. No matter how hard I tried to forget, I couldn't.

Mad. I felt like I was going mad.

"Eros!" Jasmine said, shaking Eros awake from beside me. "Eros, help her!"

Eros blinked his emerald eyes open, then suddenly sat up and grasped me, tugging me onto his lap. He rested himself against the oak headboard and slowly—very slowly—peeled my hand away from my throat. I slumped down onto his taut chest and clung onto him, my eyes closing.

It seemed like I received everyone's memories that I killed. Would I get the red-eyed woman's memories too when I killed her? Would I get to see Mom through her eyes? Mom's last few breaths, maybe?

Either way, I would find her and I would murder her, take everything she ever had and fought for. I had to kill her in honor of Mom. Mom's death wouldn't be in vain, and everyone who aided in it—even Mother—would die by my hand one of these fucking days. They all deserved it.

But I'd start with the red-eyed woman. She was somewhere in Hell, in Wrath perhaps.

"Dani, what was that?" Eros asked, pulling the silk red sheets over my body as the pink moonlight flooded in through our windows. The pressure in my esophagus slowly started to subside as he gently rubbed my neck.

I furrowed my brows, not wanting to remember that nightmare, and grasped onto him tightly, my claws digging into his back and his fingers trailing against my sides. He rocked us back and forth, as Jasmine went to retrieve a glass of tea.

"I killed so many people, Eros," I whimpered quietly, careful not to wake Lucifer. "So many people are dead because of *me*. And that's not something I could ever erase. I can't give back those lives. They'll haunt me forever. I'm just like that woman who killed my mother. I'm no better."

Eros shushed me and gently kissed my ear. "You're nothing like that woman. She killed your mother out of rage. You killed those demons to protect yourself and your kingdom. If you didn't, you'd be dead by now or spending the rest of your eternal life in a cage."

"But—"

Jasmine walked back into the room, clicked the door shut behind her, and sat at the edge of our bed, placing the glass of tea to my lips. "It'll calm you down. You'll be able to sleep for tonight without any more dreams or nightmares."

I took the glass hesitantly, my fingers trembling, and looked up at Eros.

"You need sleep, Dani. We have the meeting with the commanders in a few hours. Drink up and forget about those lost souls. What's done is done. And what you did was needed for our survival."

CHAPTER 11

A cup of tea, pink sunlight, and Sathanus's blazing red eyes really were the loveliest ways to start the day. I walked into Lust's meeting room, which sat alongside our war room, and smiled at a furious Sathanus and the six other commanders.

Honestly, I thought that this meeting was uncalled for and definitely unnecessary, but the commanders wanted to chat about the crowning ceremony. And, no matter what they said, I was prepared to defend myself. Everything that happened there happened for a reason.

Sitting at my designated seat, I glanced around the eggshell colored walls and admired the nude mosaics taken all around Hell, then finally turned my attention to Sathanus who went on and on and on about something I had done to him, screaming at me through his jagged yellow teeth.

"What was that?" I asked, completely spaced out.

I had too much other damn shit on my mind than to listen to him yell.

Lucifer sat at the head of the table, tilting his horns away from Sathanus and chuckling. Sathanus curled his barbed tail around the leg of the table and seethed at him, fume nearly smoking from his ear. I snickered at Lucifer, unable to hold it back.

"Do you two think that this is funny?" Sathanus asked. "People are dead because of *you*. My son is dead. Demons from my kingdom are dead. And you fucking laugh about it? You're not fit to be a commander."

The Greed Queen sat to Sathanus's left, adorned in the shiniest diamonds. "Says the man who kills people for fun." She rolled her golden eyes and turned back to the table. "We're not here to talk about the killings. Everyone who died deserved it. We are here to talk about Dani losing control."

"Actually, I'm here to address the people Dani killed from my kingdom," Queen Envy said, glaring at me with her piercing green eyes. She flared her nostrils and dug her fake nails into the table. "Those were some of my best warriors that you killed."

Lucifer leaned forward. "If they were your best warriors under your control, they should know how to behave at a public event, they shouldn't have beaten a human in Lust lands, and they certainly should take orders from *you*. So, are you going to let us infer that *you* were the one who called for Dani's head?"

I drew my tongue across my lower lip. "Because I can definitely take care of that now."

Suddenly nervous, Envy shook her head and pressed her green-painted lips together.

In the corner of the table, the Sloth and Gluttony princes passed a blunt back and forth. "Ya know, I think this whole thing has been blown waaaaay out of proportion," Sloth said, puffing on his joint. "Why don't we all go back to our kingdoms and smoke it out."

Greed rolled her gold eyes. "For Hell's sake, where are your parents? Why do they always send you two to our commander meetings?"

"Because they're stupid and not worth their time," Gluttony said.

"Because they rather sit on their asses all day and stuff their face," Lucifer corrected, turning back to focus his icy gaze on Sathanus. "Now, where were we? About to watch Sathanus explode again?" He kicked one leg over the other and leaned back. "Because I have been needing a good laugh."

Sathanus slammed his palms onto the table and postured over it, muscles in his red arms tensing. I flared my nostrils so damn tired of him already today and matched his glare, standing up and baring my fangs. "Sit down and shut up, Sathanus." My claws cut into the table. "Before I make you, just as I made your son."

Those voices nearly took control of me again, pleading with me to do it already. Sathanus had been the root cause of so many of my problems. If only I could fix him with one simple, short kiss. Everything would be peaceful then.

Glaring at me for a few moments, Sathanus grumbled to himself and sat down. I postured over the other commanders, smaller than everyone but damn confident in myself and my abilities. "Now, we either talk about the crowning ceremony or about the war that we will face against *Mother* soon. I suggest the latter, so we don't get fucked."

After muttering under their breath, the commanders nodded and turned their attention to me, waiting for me to continue because apparently nobody else had heard or cared much about this coming war that could kill hundreds of thousands of demons, but they had to make a huge deal out of me killing a couple. *Definitely made sense.* Not.

"According to Belial's prophecy--"

"Those prophecies are nonsense," Sathanus said, nostrils flared. "Nobody believes them."

"Don't get angry that you're not involved in it," Lucifer said, sprawling his hands down on the table. "The prophecy is true, and when war comes down upon the Earth, we must rise and be prepared. Mother will finally fall like the rest of us. Isn't that what we have all wanted for the past thousands of years?"

For the first time tonight, all the commanders actually came to an agreement. When Heaven descended upon the Earth and Hell rose, we would expose Mother for who she really was: a cold-hearted, power-hungry bitch.

CHAPTER 12

"Thanks for the Fervor Crisps, Annen!" Eros shouted over his shoulder.

We carried out a box of freshly baked goods into Chastion and walked around after my meeting with the commanders. I wouldn't say that the meeting was technically beneficial, but it got us all on the same page about the coming war, though Sathanus and Lucifer still bickered by the end of it.

I bit into a baked treat, my mouth exploding with sweet goodness, and followed the white stone through the town. Taking Eros's hand, I rested my head on his shoulder and let the pink sun warm my face. Lust demons walked around with each other, some skipping to the Garden of Roses, others sauntering to Rebel, the giant sex club that seemed to be open during all hours of the night.

"I keep having nightmares," I admitted to Eros quietly, not wanting to relive the memories but needing to get it off my chest. There wasn't much that I could hold in any longer. Between the constant voices in my head, what I did during the crowning ceremony, and the thoughts about those burning red eyes, I kept feeling worse.

Eros brushed his thumb across my knuckles and kissed my head, lips covered in white powder from the Fervor Crisps. "About what?"

"What I did to all those demons… Mom's killer and her evil red eyes," I whispered. My stomach tightened, pain shooting through me. "I want them to stop so bad, Eros… I've been having nightmares of that woman since my mother died. Hundreds of terrorizing dreams."

After pulling out another baked good, Eros guided us over to a fountain. I sat on the edge, dipping my fingers into the pink water and slouching forward, feeling the weight of the world grounding me. If I could just eliminate her from this world, maybe I could sleep a bit better.

I hated seeing those devilish eyes in my dreams every night. I wanted her to be gone, for good. And I knew just the person I needed to talk to about who she may be.

Biast Sathanus, Prince of Wrath and King of the Annoying Pricks.

CHAPTER 13

If I hated anything more than Sathanus, it was travelling to Wrath itself. Between the fire, the ash, and the horrid screams from humans, I preferred to stay away from the kingdom as much as I could. But I needed to talk to Biast now. This couldn't wait any longer.

As soon as I stepped out of the portal, the dry and arid air slithered around my throat, nearly suffocating me. Wilted leaves pitifully hung off the brittle trees, falling away when I walked by them toward the Gates to Wrath.

Children with sharp red horns and vexed stares pushed by me as they ran from the kingdom. I stepped off the busy cobblestone walkway and made a beeline for the gates, which separated the fiery kingdom from smaller towns and villages around it.

Two demons with red curved horns and black eyes guarding the entrance stared down at me when I approached them. "Commander of Lust," one sneered, baring those long jagged teeth at me. "What is a whore like you doing here?"

I crossed my arms over my chest to suppress that growing urge to kill them for their disrespect. Something told me to leave now before any of this could escalate, because once I made it into the kingdom, all kinds of demons would be after me.

"I'm here to see Biast."

The other demon chuckled menacingly at me. "Biast? What do you want with him?"

Suddenly Biast appeared behind the man, snatched him by the back of his neck—his long red talons threatening to sink into his throat—and pulled him into the air. "The lady said she was here for me, not for your prick-ish remarks," Biast growled in the demon's ear.

Dripping in fear so strong that I could sense it, the man worriedly shook his head. "It won't happen again, Lord Biast. I promise you with my life. It won't happen again," he said almost too nervously.

Biast pulled him higher into the air and sneered up at the man. "This is the second time it's happened," he seethed at him, his tail slowly curling up the demon's leg. "And last time you promised your life."

"Spare me, Biast. I have done nothing wrong. I—"

Before the demon could finish, Biast shot the jagged end of his tail straight through the man's body and out through the top of his head. My eyes widened, and I stepped back, overcome with both fear and thick, sultry desire.

Biast let the man drop to the ground and retracted his tail, catching the blood on his finger and sucking it into his mouth. "Your arousal doesn't mix well with the taste of blood, Dani. Be careful," he said, narrowing his eyes at me. "Any more and you'll be too tempting to pass up."

"I need to talk to you. Alone," I said, crossing my arms and pressing my legs together.

Biast turned to the other demon guarding the door. "Clean him up and don't tell my father about this," he said, cracking a cruel smirk and walking toward me. "If you do, your ass is next." Biast snatched my hand and pulled me away from the gates and entrance to the kingdom. "You have some balls coming to Wrath alone when my father wants to kill you."

Biast led me down an arid path toward the rivers of lava and the River of Tartarus. Bones drifted down the river, brittle and fleshless. I followed after him, taking it all in because I hadn't been down these parts before.

"Don't speak until we cross the river. Envies are known to hang out just outside of kingdoms, fishing for gold and gossip from travellers." Biast stepped right into the lava as if it didn't affect him and held out his hand for me to cross with him.

My eyes widened at his ridiculousness. "If I step in there, I'll burn."

Was he insane or just plain crazy? I didn't know how deep the river was and it was nearly fifteen feet wide. I couldn't just walk right through it. And… I didn't know how to use my wings yet.

"Come on," he said. "You won't burn."

Without taking his hand, I glared at him for another moment and inched closer to the edge, letting my toes dip into the lava. Immediately I jumped back and cradled them, watching the flesh nearly burn off to the bone.

"What the fuck is wrong with you?" I seethed. "Do you want to see me dead too?"

Biast rolled his eyes and walked out of the river, the lava rolling off him like water did when I stepped out of the ocean. He scooped me up into his arms and held me tight to his chest, his fingers curling into my sides. I flailed in his hold, trying so desperately to get out of it.

"Biast, let me out! Stop it! You're going to fucking kil--"

Biast dunked—yes, *dunked*—us both underneath the lava. I scrambled, trying to stay as close to him as possible. And yet while I was touching him, I didn't burn. None of my flesh melted away and down the river and my bones weren't boiling for someone's stew.

After a moment, Biast came up for air. My legs were wrapped

around his waist, my arms around his shoulders, my head buried in the crook of his neck. He laid one hand on my thigh and the other on my hips and continued to the other side.

I peeked my head up, noticing the position we were in and how close I was pressed against him, and sucked in a deep breath. "Holy Hell, I didn't die."

He chuckled against me and set me down on the other side of the river. "Why don't you trust me?" he asked, glancing down at my *clothes* that had definitely melted away.

I stood bare to him, pinched my lips together, and tried to cover myself with my hands. "What are you waiting for? Take off your damn shirt and give it to me," I said through clenched teeth.

For once, Biast cracked a smile at me and rocked back on his heels, eyes drifting down my body. "I prefer you this way, actually, Commander," he said, crossing his arms—his muscles flexing.

I balled my hands up into fists and yanked on his seemingly lava-proof shirt. "Give it."

Biast slowly peeled his shirt off his red, ripped abdomen and tossed it over to me. I tore my gaze away from him, vowing not to even think about the way he'd feel against me, and pulled his shirt over my head, letting it come down to my knees.

I marched through the deserted lands. "What was that?" I asked him. "How'd you make it so I didn't burn in the lava? And, you know, I didn't see any of those Envies on the way here. I'm thinking you just did that so you could see me naked."

Biast chuckled. "If I wanted to see you naked, I could do that in another way."

My cheeks flushed, breath hitching at the thought.

No, Dani, we are not thinking this way. Not at all.

"So?" I asked, crossing my arms and continuing through the desolate lands. "Did you do something to me to make it so I didn't burn? Did you cast a spell or curse me or something?"

Biast hummed in response, muscles flexing under Wrath's

blazing red sun. "Not something you'd really want to know about, seeing that you have your hands full with Eros, Lucifer, and Jasmine—if that's her name."

I cut my eyes to him. "What's that supposed to mean?"

Biast drew his forked tongue across his teeth, and I imagined it inside of—

No, I didn't. I didn't.

I shook my head to get rid of the thought and decided to let it go already. I had come here for information, and I planned to get it as soon as I could. I grabbed his arm and stopped him from moving. "I need information on a red-eyed assassin from Wrath. Tell me everything that you know."

"You're looking for a red-eyed assassin?" Biast asked, blowing out an annoyed breath through his nose. "That's why you came here? Why you risked your damn life to come alone to the Kingdom of Wrath?"

Suddenly he seemed so cold and so irate, as he stared at me with those blazing red eyes. He pressed his lips together, the outline of his jagged teeth plastered against the skin above his lips. After balling his hands into tight fists, he turned away from me.

I furrowed my brows together. "What's wrong? Why are you angry?"

"I'm not fucking angry, Dani."

Yet everything about him told me that he was.

I grasped his hand, hoping that touch would calm him down, but he snatched it out of my hold and stepped away from me giving me the cold shoulder, which was worse than him glaring me down with those cruel eyes.

After moments of silence, he growled. "There are a hundred thousand people in Hell, more than half of which are in Wrath, who have red blazing eyes and kill people. You're going to have to be a bit more specific," he seethed.

Deciding that we weren't going to get much farther with Biast being pissy, I sat down and leaned against a dried up tree. The scorching sun blazed down upon us, making me sweat. I leaned my head back against the trunk and blew out a deep breath.

"I don't have much else," I said, pressing my lips together so they wouldn't quiver. "Just that she was hired by Lust to kill Asmodeus's wife—my mom." I hugged my knees to my chest. If he didn't have any information on her, I'd be back at square one, lost and without any direction.

Mom's death would never be avenged, and I would carry this guilt for the rest of my endless life. I needed some kind of information, so I could sleep peacefully at night. After that damn nightmare, I knew that woman was after me next.

"Are you crying?" Biast asked me, glancing over his shoulder.

I glared up at him and pushed my tears away. "Screw you."

Once I stood back up, I wiped the dust from my—Biast's—shirt. "If you don't have any information or don't want to help me, fine. Get me back across the river and I'll never bother you again. And I'll give you this stupid fucking shirt back too." I stomped toward the river with my arms crossed over his chest.

But I stopped when I realized he wasn't following. I turned on my heel and raised my brows to give him that *"Well? Are you coming?"* glare. He tilted his head to the side just an inch and dropped his scowl.

"I'll get you information, but you have to do something for me," he said.

"What?"

"Similar to the party the Kingdom of Lust has every November, Wrath has an annual dinner party in January. Accompany me. After the party I'll give you everything you want to know," he said like it was nothing, as if he didn't just warn me that coming to Wrath would get me killed.

"Are you crazy?!" I asked, shaking my head. "Do you hear what you're asking me? Your father hates—more like, *loathes* —me. He will never accept me into his castle or at his party, especially not with his son. Why do you want me to come with you?"

"I want to piss him the fuck off and..." He paused. "I want to make some Envy jealous."

An Envy? I scrunched my nose, a fiery warmth spreading through my entire body. What did he want to do with an Envy? He was a dick, an asshole even, but he could do better than a damn Envy.

"You like Envies?" I asked, licking my lips. An urge to rip whoever it was apart ran through my body. "Who is she?" I asked, almost sounding possessive or... jealous.

Was I jealous? *No, I couldn't be.* Why the hell would I be jealous of an Envy?

"What's it to you?" Biast asked, curling his barbled and bloody tail around my ankle and letting it slither up my leg to just above my knee. "Do you have a problem with me going out with an Envy? I thought Lusts never get jealous, especially for people they're not in a relationship with."

I pressed my thighs together to stop his tail from moving any higher. "I'm not jealous."

"Well, then, you don't have a problem going, do you?"

"Why me?"

Biast paused, a look that I couldn't quite decipher stretching across his face. But, then, he said, "Because you're the sexiest woman in all of Hell. Who wouldn't be jealous of you? So... will you do it?"

"I'll do it..." Because I needed to find all the information about this red-eyed assassin.

One night with Biast's family wouldn't kill me, right?

"Now, was that all you fuckin' came for?" Biast asked me, his tail tightening around my inner thigh. Its barbed edges sunk into my flesh, almost to the point of breaking my skin and turning it pink and blotchy.

I gulped and shifted from foot to foot to relieve the pressure between my legs. Biast touched me like he owned me, like I was his and only his. Something about that man made me crave more from him.

Sure, Eros had been rough with me, had wrapped his hand around my throat and tugged on my hair until I screamed for him, but he hadn't made anything painful and had never drawn blood. From the thick scent of his arousal and from the way he so savagely sucked the blood of those demons at my crowning ceremony, I knew Biast liked it. Scratch that, he loved it.

"No," I lied. "I wanted to visit Wrath."

Biast growled under his breath. "You're lying."

"Show me around… or are you too afraid of your father?"

"I'm not fucking afraid of him, but you should be."

I stepped toward him and gazed up into his eyes. "I'm not afraid of your father and I'm certainly not afraid of you either. So, show me around Wrath's city or around here," I said, nodding to the River of Tartarus. It must've gone on for miles and was the same river that Beliel had traveled down from Dad's journal.

Biast looked at the space between us, retracted his tail, and stormed down the side of the river. "If you're coming, you better keep the fuck up, *Commander*, because I'm not waiting for your slow ass."

Following after him, I gazed down into the orange lava. "So, Wraths are lava and fire-proof?" I asked myself with a smile. I actually thought it was kind of… funny knowing that a Wrath could just walk through one of the most devastating substances to humans, like it was nothing.

"Some Wraths live in the fire and underneath lava around the kingdom."

"They do?" I asked, stopping and staring down into the bubbling lava.

Biast placed his hand on my shoulder and shoved me toward the lava, his fingers gripping my skin. Toes just about to touch the blazing liquid, I shouted, grasped his hand, and stumbled back into him until my back was pressed against his chest. "What is your problem today?"

"I like to hear you scream," he said. Biast trailed his large and calloused hand down my bare arm, grasped my hand, and leaned down with me to sink it into the water. "When you feel something tickle your palm, curl your hand into a fist."

I tensed and tried to move away. "Why? I don't want anyone to grab my hand."

"Nothing will happen to you."

"Says the man whose father wants him to kill me."

"Just do it, Dani."

After grumbling to myself, I sunk my hand lower into the lava river and closed my eyes, inhaling Biast's thick scent. Breath on my neck, fingers almost intertwined with his, tail curled softly around my ankle, he swore in my ear and rested his other hand on my hip.

I sucked in a breath at our closeness and suddenly felt something tickle my palm. I snapped my hand closed and pulled it from the lava, stepping away from Biast as quickly as I could because he was too damn close. All I could feel was him against my backside and his scent making me… excited the same way I had been during the crowning.

Except I couldn't steal his soul like I could the others on that night. He had been the one person who I couldn't take, the one person my angel or demon either wouldn't accept or *couldn't* accept. Or maybe we were something else to each other.

Biast clenched his jaw and grabbed my wrist. "Open your palm."

While I expected these Wraths to be lava-proof zombies or skeletons, they were much smaller and so much cuter. I opened my palm to see a charcoal covered spotted shell. After a couple moments, an orange head sprung out of it.

"Is it a turtle?" I asked.

Biast snatched the turtle by its shell, placed it on his bare chest, and sat down beside the lava. The turtle *crawled* up the side of his chest to his shoulder and plopped down like a cat would on someone's lap. "We call them roqs."

I sat down beside him, closer than I damn well expected myself to sit, and let the *roq* climb from his shoulder to mine. It felt warm, hot, almost fiery against my skin. With big bug-like eyes, the roq looked up at me and licked my neck. I laid on my back and stared up at Wrath's fiery skies as some ash rained down upon us.

"Have you heard of the prophecy about the end of Heaven and Hell as we know it?"

Biast laid down beside me, one leg outstretched and the other bent. "Yes, it's been mentioned around Wrath," he said. "But my father loves to keep his shitty Satanic religion at the forefront of everything. Prophecies like that blow right past all those mindless Satan worshippers."

"Well, Belial—the first angel who fell from Heaven—spoke about it. She was last spotted around Tartarus. Nobody has seen her for the past thousands of years. I wondered if there were more clues to the prophecy that we haven't quite found yet," I said, not wanting to admit to him that *he* was part of the prophecy.

The Beginning of the End had commenced at my crowning ceremony.

Three demons will rise from the ashes: *The Devil, The Beast, The False Prophet.* The devil was Lucifer, watching as everything occurred. The beast was Biast, who had drunk the blood of demons. The false prophet was *me,* who had sucked the souls of the innocent.

"It happened at the crowning ceremony. The beginning of the end, I mean…" I blew out a deep breath and closed my eyes, feeling such sorrow yet so much excitement at the thought of it. "When I took all those souls as if it were nothing. That's when we were doomed for eternity."

Though I felt like the entire world was crashing down upon me, though I still heard Javier every now and then accompanied by the hundreds of demons I had killed, I wasn't going to make the same mistake and hold this all inside of me. I needed to talk to someone about this.

I just couldn't believe that this *someone* was Biast.

I should've run away when I had the chance, should've told him to take me back through the lava and to the portal, yet I stayed and continued to lie next to him because something felt... well, I didn't have any other word for it except: right.

Something should've felt terribly wrong. But it didn't.

So, I laid there and I told him my worst fears, my nightmares, and more about the prophecy that my father wrote about in his journal, losing track of time and wasting the day away with a boy from a neighboring kingdom.

"Dani!" Jasmine shouted from across the lava. "Is that you?"

I opened my eyes and looked over at Biast who had sat up. The suns had set a long time ago, but the ash still fell from the sky like snow. I sat up, leaning slightly against Biast to look over at Jasmine. Jasmine's gaze lingered on Biast for a moment longer than it should've in an angry stare, then she turned back to me. "Come quick. It's Dr. U."

CHAPTER 14

"What happened to Dr. U?" I asked, following Jasmine through the hallways toward Dr. U's room. If Jasmine had traveled all the way to Wrath just to find me, it must've been bad. I hadn't had much of a chance to catch up on Dr. U's health recently and didn't want to regret not seeing her.

Kasey paced back and forth in the hallways, with her emerald gaze fixed on the ground and her arms crossed over her chest. Mycah and Aarav stood off to the side, chatting with each other. While I wanted to smile and rush over to them for being here, I stopped myself short. They probably hated me as much as Kasey did.

Yet Mycah gave me a small smile, then quickly looked away. Kasey stopped right in front of Dr. U's door as if she was guarding it from me and, suddenly, wrapped her arms around my shoulders and pulled me toward her. "You're here. She's been asking for you."

Taken by surprise and feeling beyond awkward, I gently patted her on the back and then moved away from her as Eros stepped out of Dr. U's room. He gave me one look, then glanced at Biast behind me. "You were in Wrath?" His gaze flickered down my body to Biast's t-shirt. "Without clothes?"

Biast straightened his back and crossed his arms, glaring at Eros. "She fell into the lava pits," Biast said, as if he didn't almost drown me in them. "Don't worry. We didn't *fuck* if that's what you're worried about, but that doesn't mean that she didn't want—"

I elbowed Biast hard in the rib cage because I didn't want him to say it out loud. I hated him with every fiber of my being and I would never go back on that. Biast and I were never to be together, maybe in fighting the evils in this world, but *not* in a relationship.

That's the lie I told myself today.

After I ordered Biast to find me some pants, I moved toward Eros to grasp his hand. "Is she okay? Tell me that Dr. U is okay."

Eros took another long look at Biast. While I usually could tell exactly what he was thinking, I couldn't find the words. It wasn't lust, nor anger, nor even jealousy. I wanted to ask him, but I had some more important matters at hand.

When he tugged me into the room, I stopped dead in my tracks and gulped. Just like Trevon, Dr. U looked bad—worse even, as she laid in the bed and stared up at the ceilings with black eyes and paling skin, frail arms, and skinny legs.

"Dani," Dr. U said, reaching out to me with a weak hand. It seemed as if the wounds and injuries that those Envies caused had only gotten worse. Bruises decorated her arms, those bright eyes were swollen shut, she looked so... so tired and broken.

She grasped my hand and pulled me closer to her. "Tell me what's wrong. You look exhausted," she whispered, her voice dry.

I knelt by her side and brushed my fingers against her cheek. "There is nothing wrong," I whispered, tucking some thin hair behind her ear. The wrinkles on her face had seemed to become even more pronounced, her body thinning at an astronomically unhealthy pace. "Nothing."

"You're a terrible liar."

She had picked up on it quicker than I thought. I wanted to tell her the truth: that part of me felt numb after killing all those people. I both loved and loathed the feeling of taking someone's soul because they all deserved it but their families didn't. I had always been that good girl who gave people way too many chances; this lust for more was almost too much to handle.

After giving her my best smile, I shook my head. "It doesn't matter about me right now. We have to focus on you getting better, then we can sit in hours of therapy together and you can pick apart my brain."

She gently grasped my cheek and then dropped her hand as if it weighed too much to hold upright. "Dani," she said, voice hoarse. "I'm getting worse. My body feels weak. I... I'm sorry for all this. I don't want you to worry about me too. You have so much going on."

"Stop it," I said to her, shaking my head as tears welled up in my eyes. Light flooded into the room through the curtains and illuminated her face. "You're the most important person to me. You're not a nuisance." I grasped her fragile hand.

"But Dani..."

"Stop it right now. I don't want to hear it."

"Dani," the doctor called. "Can I speak to you?"

After kissing Dr. U on the forehead, I hurried into the hallway where Mycah and Aarav were comforting Kasey, and Biast was leaning against the wall with a pair of pants in his hand. He tossed them to me, muttering some sort of annoyance under his breath, and I pulled them on.

"Why isn't she getting any better?" I asked him, narrowed my eyes and felt the rage boil within me.

"We've run some tests. The Envies had done more than just beat her. They injected her with a drug that slowly starts to shut down a human's organs. It's originally made in Wrath and is used to torture mortals in Hell."

"They used Broth of Despair on her?" Biast asked, suddenly looking concerned. Despite his natural pink skin, he looked extremely pale as if this was dangerous and couldn't be fixed. He kicked himself off the wall and moved closer to me. "It's... fatal."

The doctor cleared his throat and frowned at me. "Nothing can fix it. Once it has been inserted into the bloodstream, the potion takes control of the body and doesn't back off until the human is dead."

"That's not true," Biast said. "It can be reversed with the blood of a true demon."

After furrowing his brows, the doctor glanced over at Biast. "I've never heard of such a thing," he said to me with a shake of his head. "It has never been done before. I have never seen it."

I glanced up at Biast with big, hopeful eyes. "Are you being serious?" I whispered.

Once he looked down at me, he nodded. "Yes."

If this was the only way to save Dr. U, then it had to be done. "I'll do it."

"You're half-angel," Biast said, flicking his forked red tongue. "Your blood will just make it worse. We need someone with a hundred percent demon blood."

Kasey stepped forward. "Me. I'll be the one to save her. I can't bear to see her this way."

Everyone suddenly got quiet, and the doctor looked at me as if it was *my* choice to make. Dr. U was under my care and had been like a mother to me since childhood. But did I want Kasey to save her? What if this was another one of Kasey's tricks? What if she wanted Dr. U dead to weaken me?

Eros gave me his best grimace and shrugged. "If it could work..."

I turned on my heel toward Kasey. "If this is some plot to hurt me, I will kill you without a second thought or care. Dr. U's life is in danger. Don't play with me like this."

"I'm not," Kasey said with wide green eyes. "I truly care about her."

Though I was still hesitant, if this was the only way, then this was what we would have to do. I wouldn't let another person I cared about die by the hand of a demon.

After the doctor, Kasey, and Dr. U left to prepare for the blood transfusion, I paced up and down the hallway as Biast and Eros stared at each other from opposite seats. My nerves were through the roof. I didn't want Dr. U to die. She was really the only family that I had left.

If she departed from this world, all this would be for nothing.

I plopped down in the seat next to Eros and closed my eyes, hoping for the best.

"So," Eros said after sticking his hands into his pockets, his cinnamon scent drifting through my nose and calming me only slightly. "You didn't tell me about Biast."

Nervously tapping my foot on the floor of the waiting room, I glanced over at Biast who sat across from us, with his usual pissed-off fiery stare and his barbed tail curled around a chair leg, his long sanguine-colored talons strumming against his thigh. When he lifted his gaze to meet mine, I looked back at Eros, grasped his hand, and rested my head on his shoulder.

"Nothing happened between us. I went to Wrath to ask him about the woman who killed my mother," I said to him honestly.

"What'd he tell you?"

After shifting uncomfortably beside Eros, I tensed. "He said that he'll find any information that he can and get back to me after the infamous dinner party that his kingdom hosts every year... the one I'm attending," I said, whispering the last part.

"You're going to their party?"

"It's the only way he'll give me any information."

Eros tensed beside me and shook his head. "Sathanus will try to kill you."

"He might try but he won't succeed."

Biast tapped his fingers against the chair handle, the sound making me nervous. I glanced from him to the hospital room and growled under my breath. "Quit it or leave," I snapped. It was bad enough I had to spend the night with that man in a couple days, but I didn't want to listen to him tap his fingers over and over and over against the wooden chair.

Instead of snapping back at me, Biast stood and walked down the hallway, the muscles in his back flexing through his thin shirt. I looked at Eros and patted his knee. "Nothing will happen, I promise. Biast would kill his father before he tried to kill me."

"You truly think that?" Eros asked, giving me a skeptical look. "Because last time that Biast took control of Trevon's body he *did* try to kill you, multiple times."

"Actually, I was the only one who calmed his demon," I said, staring at the now empty seat in front of me. "But, yes, I think that he'd keep me safe." I didn't know how I knew that, but I did. The way that Biast was looking at me at the lava river this morning told me more than I needed to know about him. It wasn't hard to miss. "He hates his father, almost more than I do."

Eros leaned back, wrapped an arm around the back of my seat, and sighed. "Are you sure?" he asked me, suddenly clenching my shoulder. "Because I can't lose you." He kissed me on the cheek. "I know that I don't say it a lot, but I need you more than you know." He brushed his nose up the side of my neck. "More than you will ever fucking know."

I cuddled up close to him and turned my face towards him. "I love you," I whispered, knowing what this was really about. "Nobody will ever take your place. Nobody could *ever* replace you."

Wrapping me in his arms, Eros pulled me into his lap and

gently dug his fingers into my hips. "Good, because I wouldn't let you do that. You're mine, Dani, whether you want to be or not."

"Whether I want to be?" I asked, poking him in the stomach. "I always had wanted to be."

"Sorry to interrupt." The doctor popped his head out of the door and smiled at me. "Dani..." he said, grasping the door handle until his knuckles paled. "Dr. U will be okay. She's recovering now. Kasey's blood was a perfect match for her."

Dr. U would be okay for now, but who knew what the future would hold with all that demon blood rushing through her veins.

CHAPTER 15

Sitting up brightly in the bed, Dr. U beamed at me. Though the usual green veins under her eyes were a dark and demonic purple and her canine teeth were just a smidge sharper, she looked the same *and* she looked healthy finally, as if the blood transfusion worked almost instantly.

"I want to go home," Dr. U said to me. As she glanced over at Kasey, pink sunlight gleamed against her face. Her wrinkles seemed to have almost disappeared, Kasey's demon blood having an effect on her already. "I have been here for so long. Take me home."

Before Kasey could grab her hand, I scooped it up in mine and gently tugged her out of bed. She jumped onto her two feet, swaying for a second, then regained her balance. We walked out of the room quickly and much easier than I expected. And when I saw the empty hospital chair empty that Biast had sat in a few moments ago, my heart tugged.

I wished he would've stayed.

Shaking my head to rid myself of the thought, I followed Eros to Lust's black mystical portals. "I have some *business* to take care of here," Eros said to me before we left. "I'll see you when you get back. Don't stay out too late. I love you."

After arching my brow at whatever his *business* was, I kissed him on the cheek and walked with Dr. U through the portal to her house. It seemed like an eternity since I had last been here, but it hadn't changed one bit with the large windows that overlooked a beautiful and majestic forest.

I sat on her red suede couch and watched Dr. U glide around the living room as if she hadn't just been bed-bound for the past few days and could barely move. Everything about her seemed to come alive, though the blood inside of her was of a demon. She smiled warmly at me and took a deep breath of the fresh earthly air. Though her plants withered away, she wandered over to them and smelt each of their leaves, inhaling their scent. Everything was probably more intense for her now, as it was with all demons.

Never in my life did I expect or want her to become a demon, but Dr. U was happy and healthy for now. And that was all I could ever ask for in this life. I didn't want her to die like she had in my nightmare, taken by a ruthless demon because of her ties to angels.

Kasey shuffled by my side and smiled at Dr. U. "She's healthy."

"She is."

Kasey shifted from foot to foot. "I don't know if I told you, but we dated years ago."

"I know," I said, keeping my dialogue with her short and sweet.

I didn't trust her as much as I should've. I had let her out of the Chains, yet she still had wanted to pick a fight with me that day. She could fight with me all she wanted, but Dr. U was off limits. I hoped she knew that or else there would be consequences far worse than just some measly chains.

"Dani, I'm—"

"If you hurt her, I will kill you."

Kasey widened her green eyes. "I would never do that."

"She's the only family that I have, Kasey."

"Dani, I would never."

I glanced over at her, pressed my lips together, then looked down at my phone. I didn't have anywhere to be at the moment, but I didn't want to spend the rest of the night with Kasey, who I highly doubt would leave anytime soon. At the same time, I didn't want to just leave Kasey over here with nobody else. They had dated at one point, but—

Kasey grabbed my hands and brushed a strand of hair out of my face. "Dani, please, trust me with her. She's my old girlfriend and has helped me through so much shit. I would never hurt her and would protect her with my life. And, if I ever did hurt her, I'd probably drink enough Vemon from Pride to kill myself from guilt."

Dr. U walked over to us, placing her hands on my shoulders. "I'm fine, Dani. Don't worry about me," she said, grasping my jaw like she always did. Her hands felt harder, more calloused and rough, and somehow younger too.

"Are you sure?" I whispered.

She nodded her head. "Positive. Now, should I get us some tea? You promised me a therapy session back at the hospital."

I gave her my best half-smile. "Rain-check. I don't have the time to get into half the shit I've dealt with these past few weeks. How about next week?"

Dr. U nodded. "Next week it is."

~

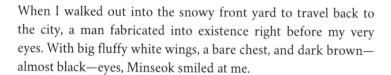

When I walked out into the snowy front yard to travel back to the city, a man fabricated into existence right before my very eyes. With big fluffy white wings, a bare chest, and dark brown—almost black—eyes, Minseok smiled at me.

"Dani," Minseok said. "We meet again."

I arched a brow at him and walked past him. "Not by coincidence…"

He followed after me, his wings brushing against my back. I stepped away and looked at all the human houses around here, then grasped his hand and pulled him behind a tree. "What the hell are you doing? Put those damn things away."

Minseok smirked at me and hiked his thumb backward toward his wings. "These?"

"Yes, those!" I pushed on the sides of them, hoping they'd shrink. "Put them away."

"Don't worry," he said to me. "Nobody but you can see them."

My brows furrowed, and I stopped short. "You're lying."

"Really," he said, cracking a smile. "Take yours out and I can show you how to do it."

My cheeks flushed red at the thought of not knowing how to even use them yet, and I continued walking, not wanting to admit that I was half angel but couldn't figure any part of my angel side out. It was beyond embarrassing.

"Don't tell me that you don't know how to use them," Minseok said, hurrying after me. When I didn't say anything, he grabbed my hand and stopped short. He pulled away almost immediately, cheeks turning a deep pink. "Sorry, but you really don't?"

I rolled my eyes at him and crossed my arms over my chest. "No, I don't. But I know how to use my teeth," I said, showing him my fangs. "If you touch me again, I'll sink them into your lips and suck out your soul… Unless that's what you want."

Minseok looked down at my fangs, gulped, and glanced back up at me. After shaking his head, he replaced his unsure smile with a genuine one. "Let me teach you how to use them. It's the least I could do after what happened to your mentor down in Hell."

Though I didn't want to trust him, at some point I needed to learn how to use my wings. I could ask Eros, but he hadn't had wings for thousands of years and I didn't want to bring up any bad memories with them anymore.

"Five minutes," I said to him. "No longer. I have places to be."

Lie.

He went to grab my hand but pulled himself away before he could touch me. Then he started through the woods, until we came to a clearing that didn't have any houses or any people near. He stretched his wings as far as they could go, and while they were enormous, they weren't as big as mine were.

Eros said that he didn't even think Lucifer had as grand of wings as me.

Minseok walked behind me and brushed his fingers against the center of my back where my wings had sprouted at one point. He got close, almost so close that the hairs on my arms stuck up. He cleared his throat. "Close your eyes and clench the muscles in your back, right here."

Though weary, I closed my eyes and clenched the muscles where he had touched.

One moment passed. Then two. Even three. And nothing happened.

"It's not working."

"Stay calm, Dani. You're getting yourself all worked up. It will never work like this."

I furrowed my brows together and blew out a deep breath, clenching again. "It's not."

He placed his hands on my shoulders and moved closer to me. "Calm down," he whispered into my ear, the sound of his breathing making me a nervous wreck. He was too close, too damn close.

Yet I blew out another deep breath to relax myself. A dull ache split through my back. I focused my attention on it, relaxing further and further until I felt like I was floating. I slowly opened my eyes to see myself floating yards in the air, almost at the top of the trees with Minseok in front of me, smiling.

"How do you feel?" he asked.

My lips curled into a small smile. "Good," I whispered.

I had finally done it, albeit with the help of an angel. But I did it nonetheless. It was a power that I knew I'd use against Minseok one day soon in the war that would be known for ages.

Floating in the sky for another hour with Minseok, I twirled, somersaulted, even danced on the air, loving this freeing feeling rushing through my veins. And, then, when the sky darkened around us, I drifted back down to the earth and retracted my wings, knowing that I couldn't stay much longer.

"Well, I have to go," I said to Minseok, shivering slightly. "It was, uh, good seeing you again, I guess. Thanks for the new talent."

Snow drifted down from the skies, the chilly air nearly freezing off my toes. Those lava pits with Biast seemed pretty nice right now. And when I went to walk away, Minseok grabbed my wrist and pulled me back. Somehow, his hands felt even colder on my bare skin, as if they had been chilled for centuries upon centuries. At first, I thought it was just the coldness that was winter, but his hands felt like they were chilled down to the bone.

"Dani, have you thought about what I asked you a few days ago? About Trevon?"

As he said Trevon's name, I yanked my hand away and pushed my shoulders back. I hadn't had much time to go see him as much as I wanted to. It had only been a few days since the burning started, but… it didn't matter. Trevon was still dying. Which meant that demons had fucked up *two* friends of mine.

"He's getting worse," Minseok continued, tugging me toward the trees. "We're keeping up with his condition."

"He doesn't need your help," I seethed at him.

Minseok swayed his hand in a circular motion and a portal-looking image appeared before us. It was of Maria's apartment and of Trevon laying helplessly on the couch. His brown skin had turned a deep red color, searing and sizzling still.

All the blood drained from my face. I swallowed hard and tore my gaze away from the image. Surely, he wasn't that bad yet. And, if he was, then why hadn't Mother helped yet? If she was oh-so-holy and kind like all the angels believed she was, she wouldn't have even thought about letting one of her own die. She would've taken him up to Heaven and healed him already.

But she wasn't who they thought she was. She was a monster.

I didn't need Eros or Lucifer to tell me. I knew it. She had let Mom die. She had let me be an orphan. She was letting Trevon burn because a demon had possessed him. She was no kind woman, she was evil. Pure evil.

"Tell me, Minseok..." I balled my hands into fists and stepped away from him, feeling the wrath and rage pump through me. I must've been hanging out with Biast too much. "Why does *Mother* not help him now? If she's so loving and caring and holy, she should care for her *child*. But she lets him burn and gives me an ultimatum instead."

A look of uncertainty crossed Minseok's face, as if he had never even thought about it before. Then, just as quickly as it appeared, it disappeared. "I don't know what you're talking about, Dani. Mother has offered you—a demon—to come to Heaven to talk with her. You should be thankful."

"Thankful?" I asked, the words tasting so sour on my tongue. "Should I be thankful that she let my mother die? Should I be thankful that I had to grow up without parents? Should I be thankful that the woman who claims to be gracious didn't want *anything* to do with me until I became Commander of Lust and her greatest enemy?"

Minseok shook his locks of thick black hair. "I don't understand your logic. Your mentor was just badly wounded by demons, and you continue to support them? Why is that, Dani? Everyone you care about is being hurt by them."

"And my mentor was healed by one too," I said, thinking back to Kasey. "At least demons have my back when I need them the most. They might be harsher than humans, but they have hearts. They aren't heartless like that woman that you call mother."

Without listening to another word, I turned on my heel and started toward the city to go back to Hell. Minseok stood in the forest watching me walk away from him. I expected him to say something, to defend mother again… but he didn't. He let me walk away until I was nearly out of sight.

"The offer still stands," he shouted.

I glanced back at him and stepped out of his line of vision, stewing in my own anger. I wondered if it was Javier backing up some rage inside of me, or maybe it was all the demons I had consumed, but I wanted to drag Minseok right into Hell with me to see if he'd see it then, that we weren't all as bad as mother said we were.

CHAPTER 16

Two days later I stood in Maria's apartment, preparing for Wrath's dinner party. Because I wanted Sathanus to hate me even more than he already did—it was fun, okay?—I dressed in the most skin-tight velvet red dress that I could find. Not only did the dress have a long split up the side, but it clung to every one of my curves and showed way more cleavage than I should've in Wrath.

Beyoncé played softly on the speaker in the living room, Maria swaying back and forth to her music while fastening a ruby necklace around my neck and letting it hang between my breasts. "You look so hot," she squealed, jumping up and down in her pajamas. "You are going to make so many people jealous, especially those Envies!"

"You think?" I asked, grabbing some lipstick and painting my lips red in the mirror.

"Duh!" Maria said. She grabbed Zane from the kitchen and marched him into the room. "Doesn't Dani look sexy? Those Envies are going to drop fucking dead when they see her, as they should."

Zane leaned against the wall, his eyes filling with dark lust. "She does."

I rolled my eyes, not wanting to return the same flirtatious look, then smirked. "Tomorrow night, I'll watch Trevon and get you dressed up like this so you and Zane can go out to the Lounge again." I winked at her reddening face, then looked back into the hallway. "How is Trevon doing? I haven't heard him complaining all night yet."

Maria and Zane exchanged a look, Maria gnawing on her lower lip. "He locked himself in your old room and kept calling out your name these past couple days. He sounded like he was in pain," Maria said, blowing out a deep breath. "He's sleeping now, so I wouldn't bother him. He sleeps relatively soundly."

Frowning, I pulled my gaze away from the hallway and leaned against the back of the leather couch. My chest tightened at the thought of not having visited Trevon these past few days. I had been so busy with preparing for this party and working closely with the doctor to find a cure for him, but… we'd come up with nothing.

Every lotion, every pill, every injection flopped.

Someone knocked on the front door, and Eros walked in, blowing out a deep breath when he saw me. "There you are," he said, taking my face in his hands and kissing me on the lips. "I thought that you were getting ready at the castle."

Fingers curling around his collar, I smiled. "Maria offered to help."

"We need to talk," he said, pulling me into the kitchen where it was a bit more private.

My brows furrowed together. "Is everything okay? Did something happen?"

"I'm not comfortable with you traveling to Wrath alone," Eros said.

I clasped a necklace around my neck with one hand, fingers

curling around the granite countertops with the other. "I won't be alone. Biast will be there."

Eros shut the door and leaned against the kitchen island bed, leaning forward to capture my hand in his. "His father wants to kill you. I don't know him and don't think that he would be able to protect you himself if his father decided to spike your drink or lean across the table to kill you. Wraths torture humans and other demons alike. Biast has done it to multiple acquaintances of mine. What makes you think that you're so different?"

I trailed my finger in soothing circles around Eros's hand. "Biast could've killed me multiple times. I had been alone with him for hours now, and he hadn't tried once. In fact…" I gnawed on the inside of my lip and remembered the last time he looked at me, really looked at me. It was more than just a look of hatred that Wraths usually had and more than a look of desire that a Lust could muster within someone.

Eros pulled me closer. "In fact, what, Dani? Don't keep things from me."

"I don't want you to get jealous," I whispered, stroking his cheek.

"Lusts don't get jealous."

I arched a hard brow at him and narrowed my eyes. "They don't get jealous? You seem to get jealous all the time."

"I'm just looking out for you."

"Are you? Or are you looking out for yourself?" I asked, getting more defensive than I should've. But Eros wanted me to go out with Lucifer for a reason and they were close, *too* damn close. I didn't think it was very fair that he didn't want me to see other people when he was doing who knew what with Lucifer behind my back. "What's going on with you and Lucifer?"

Eros tensed when I said his name. I had wanted to wait until he was ready to tell me, but I wanted to know. If they were sleeping together, I… I needed to know, because Eros had been getting awfully jealous lately, and I didn't want to be that stupid girlfriend who just let her man do whatever the hell he wanted to do without knowing who or *what* he was involved in.

If we were going to have an open relationship, we needed honesty.

Eros shook his head. "Nothing."

"He wants to sleep with you," I said to him. "Do you want to sleep with him?"

Again, Eros went quiet. Then, suddenly, he rubbed a hand over his face. "It's complicated between us, Dani. You know that."

After sighing, I stood on my toes and kissed him on the forehead. "When you're ready to talk about it more, I'll be here to listen. But, right now, I promised Biast that I'd go with him. If I don't, he won't give me any information that I need to find Mom's killer. I love you." I kissed him yet again. "I always will. If Biast tries anything, I will kill him and everyone in his family too."

CHAPTER 17

"Wrath is closed to visitors today," a guard with pointy red horns said to me in the Wrath portal room, fire blazing from his fingertips as if he was threatening to burn me if I didn't leave and head back to Lust right now.

Instead of being intimidated, I placed my hand right over his —letting the flames burn me—and put them out. "I've been invited by the Prince of Wrath, so I suggest you move out of my way before he does to you what he did to the last guard."

The Wrath scoffed. "What'd he do to the last guard?"

Biast walked through the open doors, a wave of heat following him in, and snatched the demon by the back of his neck. "You don't want to fucking find out," he said into his ear, talons digging into his throat.

Squirming in his hold, the Wrath nodded. "Yes, of course."

After Biast tossed him aside, he turned toward me with a devilish smile and blazing red eyes. "You look… so much sexier than you did at your crowning." Biast held an arm out for me, as if he wanted me to take it. "Come, we'll be late."

I wrapped my arm around his, my fingers curling into the thick red muscle, then I followed him on the path toward the castle, black ash drifting down from the gloomy gray skies. Biast ignored the whispers from his father's subjects and walked right past the guards at the main gates.

"How is that woman doing?" Biast asked.

I raised a brow and looked up into his blazing red eyes in surprise. "You mean, Dr. U? Why do you want to know about her?" I asked, brushing some ash off my velvet dress. Never in a million years did I think that he would ask me a question about her. Wraths did as they wanted, fought as they wanted, hurt as they wanted. They didn't care about anyone who wasn't family or friends.

"Forget that I asked," Biast snapped, looking down at the stony paths as they turned to smooth and shiny black obsidian.

"Kasey put her blood into her," I stated, a few moments later. "She's doing good as of right now. I checked in on her this morning and she was more lively than I had ever seen her. Thanks for asking."

When I glanced up at him, he stared down at me intensely like he actually cared or, at least, like he was actually listening to me. For some devilish reason, my cheeks heated, and I looked back down before I could stop myself.

Was I... was I blushing? Had Biast—the most aggravating demon in all of Hell—made me blush? I shook my head to myself and cursed under my breath. No, the fire pits were just making it so hot here. I wasn't used to it. I wasn't blushing because of him. And this warm fuzzy feeling in my chest definitely wasn't because of him either.

Glancing back up, I suddenly stopped and sucked in a breath. Obsidian walkways, a colossal statue of Sathanus ripping apart chains with lava pooling from his eyes and into the river below, upside down silver crosses, and a castle that spurted lava and rocks from its apex—Sathanus's palace—but it was... more than I expected it to be.

"Do you like it?" Biast asked with a smile.

"It's very fitting," I said, heart pounding a bit faster.

We continued our walk to the castle—which definitely had the same terrifying feel as the outside—in silence, never once speaking up again until after we made it into the main dining area and he curled his arm around my waist. I avoided all eye contact with any Wrath demons, not wanting to see Sathanus right now.

"So…" I rocked back on my heels and scanned the room for any sign of an Envy. "Where's that Envy you want to impress, because I don't see any here?"

Biast clenched his jaw and glanced around the room, eyes landing on the group of Envies who walked through the double doors. "The one in the center."

The one in the center was one of Kasey's friends and the daughter of the Envy Queen. It infuriated me because—despite being solely an Envy—she was absolutely beautiful with luscious soft green hair and piercing emerald eyes.

"Looks like you and her would make a good couple," I said through clenched teeth, rage rushing through me. "You're both corrupt children of even more corrupt leaders. Congrats on picking a good one."

Biast looked down at me, his tail snaking its way up and around my left leg. "Jealous?"

After nearly snorting at how ridiculous he sounded, I shook my head and walked around the room, ignoring the glares. "Why would I be jealous? I loathe you with a passion so hot that it'd burn Wrath to pieces."

After chuckling to himself, the sound unusual coming from him, he snatched my hand and led me to a door. "You're always welcome to lose control again, Dani. I wouldn't mind getting to taste all that corruption on your lips."

"Is it the corruption you want to taste, or is it me?" I asked.

Biast drew his forked tongue across his bottom lip and stayed quiet, kicking open the door and urging me outside on the balcony before dinner began. Everything around us burned, red flames licking the edges, orange lava pooling around the castle, and black ash raining down. It was my dream with Javier all over again, almost to a T.

Except instead of placing his hands on the balcony next to me and trapping me like Javier did, Biast curled his barbed tail up my thigh and tightened his grip on my waist. "It's both the corruption and you," he said to me, voice rough in my ear. "I haven't stopped craving it since your ceremony." He pushed me against the railing, my breasts pressing against the edge.

It was well over a hundred and fifty degrees here, yet his touch made me shiver.

"I'd give you everything to have another taste, Dani."

He breathed against my ear and rested his forehead against the side of mine, forcing sinful thoughts into my mind of me with a Lust crown on my head, the ruby red tips adorned with Wrath flames, and Biast by my side.

He snaked his hand around my neck from behind and gently squeezed. "Everything for another taste of you."

"Be careful with your words, Biast, unless you really mean it," I said, turning around and looking up into those beautiful eyes. "Because *everything* means everything that you have, everything you want, and everything you are. And I don't know if a demon like you is prepared for a soul-sucking woman like me."

When I walked away from him, he snatched my wrist and pulled me back, his lips centimeters from mine. "You talk a big game for a demon who hasn't even been leading her kingdom for two weeks yet."

"I don't play games, Biast," I said, wrapping my hand around his collar and leaning in closer to him, as if I was going to give him another taste. Then I pulled away from him, walked back toward the doors to the dining area, and called over my shoulder, "But I do like to tease."

CHAPTER 18

After an actual dinner from hell with Sathanus threatening to kill me every two minutes and Biast actually flirting with me, I walked out of the castle with him by my side, sweat rolling down my neck. It was too damn hot here to even think, and those damn Envies all night were the worst. Especially the one that Biast liked, apparently.

I thought he could do so much better than her, but what did I know?

"What'd your *girl* say?" I asked, lip curled into a scowl.

"What's it to you?" he asked me, forked tongue gliding across his bottom lip.

Before we left, Biast just had to go talk to her, and I definitely wasn't jealous of it. Not one bit. I was just peeved because I wanted to get out of Wrath as soon as possible. I didn't want to stand around while Sathanus and his devil worshipper Satanists walked around me with pitchforks and tried to kill me. Nope, not on my list of things to do today.

Crossing my arms, I arched a brow at Biast, then turned away, not wanting to continue the conversation about the pretty Envy with green eyes that Biast might date after tonight. Because she sure as hell was jealous and envious that I was on his arm.

"I want my information," I said to him, stepping over some burned human flesh on the walkways within the nearest town we had to pass through to get back to the portals. This shit along with upside down crosses were everywhere in Wrath, it seemed.

"We can't talk here," Biast said. "Too many prying ears."

"Fine, come back to Lust with me then. We can talk there, and I'll treat you to some Fervor Crisps."

After giving me a slight nod—so unlike Biast—he clenched his jaw and continued forward through the town towards the portals. Ever since we left the party, he had been nothing but pissed off, which I guess was usual. But his father really was annoying tonight.

"Your father treats you like shit," I said to him. "Why do you let him do that to you?"

Biast growled, his talons cutting right into the skin on his palms. "That's none of your fucking business."

I crossed my arms over my chest. "Actually, it is. If I'm going to have you as an ally, I need you to be strong and not let your father push you around like that. He's a weak and easily angered man."

"So am I," Biast snapped.

Glancing up at him, I found myself wrapping my arm around his and made him tense. "You're not weak," I whispered up into his ear. I drew my finger down his rough skin and found myself enjoying the feel of him against me. "The only thing that Sathanus has that you don't is his religion, but you don't believe in it, do you?"

"That's why he despises me," Biast said through gritted sharp teeth. "I'm not going to blindly worship him knowing who he really is. If half the demons in Wrath and Hell really knew him, they wouldn't either."

"You're stronger than Sathanus is, you know. You could just... steal his throne."

Don't make the mistake of thinking I actually wanted something good for Biast. I wanted him King and Commander, so I didn't have to think about constant war with Wrath. I would have two kingdoms under my control—sort of—and Wrath wouldn't betray me during any time, as long as Biast was on my side.

"And lead what?" Biast asked. "All his followers would be lost without him chiefing their religion."

My lips curled into a smile. "Then you lead it," I said, drawing my nails up and down his forearm. "You don't have to believe in it to blindly lead demons who will trust in anything. They want to believe in something, even if it is evil, and I know that you know evil all too well."

Biast paused, tensed, and glanced down at me. "What happened to you? You used to be a pushover who feared wrongdoing."

"Hell's corrupted me," I said.

"You weren't this foul in the beginning with Eros."

"Well, maybe it was you who corrupted me then." I stopped just as we made it out of the town and stared up into his fiery eyes. "How do you feel about that, Biast? You're the reason for my corruption, for the evil running through my veins, and for my cold, dark heart."

It was supposed to come out lighthearted but came out with nothing but... sultry desire.

Because I liked this part of me.

After staring at me for a few moments, Biast looked from my eyes to my lips, then snatched my wrist and turned away. "We have to go back to Lust. I thought you wanted your information."

Before he could move much further, I yanked him back. "I have other things I want to talk to you about too. You said that there was a reason I couldn't take your soul when I kissed you. I want to know what it is."

Biast pressed his lips together. "I already told you that you'll never find out from me."

I grabbed his hand. "Tell me why. I need to know what the connection is between us."

Wrapping his hand around my neck, he pushed me against one of the many withering charcoal trees lining the walkways toward the portal. He stared at me for a moment longer than it seemed he intended to, because he pulled his hand away and turned his back to me. "No."

I wanted to pull him back and demand to know what was between us, but he walked away—faster this time—toward the portal black doors. He ripped one open and disappeared inside the building, leaving me out here alone. Scurrying after him, I used all my strength to open that heavy door and walked to black misty portal beside Biast.

"Tell me," I said while we walked through the portal, ignoring the wailing demons inside of it. "I want to know. I *deserve* to know."

"Do you?" Biast snapped, eyes becoming two pits of darkness. "You won't fucking like it if I do tell you about it, Dani. You'll fucking despise it."

"And why would I do that?" I asked, crossing my arms and kicking off some demons who reached for my legs inside the portal. "What makes you so sure?"

Biast grabbed my throat again and pulled me closer to him. "Because nobody ever wants to be connected to someone like me," he finally growled. He shoved me away and continued toward Lust. "Now, quit it."

After catching my breath, I hurried toward him and grabbed his bicep. "No. Tell me."

Biast snarled. "You don't stop, do you?"

"No, I don't," I said. He pressed his lips together and stepped into Lust, the soft pinkish hues under the moon relaxing me. Home, I was finally home. I grabbed a Passion Delight from one of the many servants in the portal room and handed it to Biast. "Drink this and tell me."

To my surprise, Biast actually took the drink, swallowed it, and thrust the empty glass back to me a few moments later. "I've never fucking understood my father's religion. I've always fucking hated it. When I was younger, I sought out prophecies. Every fallen angel comes down to hell with one for them or for the world itself, almost as a parting gift. Not that *that woman* would ever give a fallen angel a gift."

I grabbed a glass for myself and sipped it down. It was probably the sixth of the night, which definitely wasn't a good thing, because I feared I'd make a terrible decision soon. Walking next to him down the cherry-tree lined white stone paths, I nodded along. I didn't know that everyone came down with a prophecy. Lucifer must've had one, and Eros would've had one too if he had been banished from Heaven and didn't just aimlessly follow Lucifer down here.

"I found more understanding in the prophecies than Satanism." Biast balled his hands into fists. "I have been collecting as many of them as I could find to figure out and prepare for the future. I always thought it was more important than killing people or drinking Passion Delights until you couldn't feel anymore like my brother and father. If I wanted to lead the kingdom, I needed to understand our danger."

"And what did you find?" I asked, walking up the castle steps.

The guards opened the double doors for us, and I led us to the bar area with plush pink couches. I glanced around for Eros, faintly smelling his and Lucifer's scent in the castle but not knowing where he was.

Biast nodded to the bar. "You should probably have another drink before I tell you."

Arching a brow, I scurried behind the bar and made myself another one because... Biast smelled too good. And if I did anything with him, I could blame the alcohol and my insane horniness on Passion Delights.

"Alright," I said, careful not to slosh the drink over the side of the cup.

After I sat on the couch beside him, he stared at me for a few moments, then tore his gaze away, completely pulling himself away from me. "The child of the first commander of Wrath is destined to be with a Queen of Lust."

Eyes widening, I swallowed hard and placed the drink on the glass table in front of us, my heart racing with… anxiety, or maybe that was excitement. Whatever the feeling, it was similar to how I felt during my crowning when I sucked soul after soul out of guilty demons.

"I never thought that it would be about me," Biast said, staring out the large windows. "Only the first children typically marry the first children of other kingdoms, to provide their sub-kingdom with powerful leadership. But Javier's dead, and I think that it's… us."

"Us?" I whispered. "Because I couldn't suck out your soul?"

Biast peered over at me, his tail curled around my ankle slightly. "Yes."

Rage rushed through me, and I smacked him on the shoulder. "You were going to let me kill you if you were wrong?"

Though I expected Biast to push me off him, like his angry ass usually did, he let me hit him and I didn't stop. My hands felt so good on his body that I crawled on top of him, smacking him and waiting for an answer. Biast set his hands on my thighs, eyes fading slightly.

"Was it your plan to get me so drunk off Passion Delights that I-I—" I started, slurring my words and drunk off his scent. I inhaled deeply as heat warmed my core, gathering and building, pushing me higher until I needed some sort of a release. Maybe it was a mix of the way he smelled, the lust, the connection between us. I didn't know. But I wrapped my hand around the back of his neck, pulled him closer to me, and closed my eyes. "Until I wanted you? Until I couldn't keep my hands off you, Biast, after you told me the truth? Because…" I leaned closer to breathe in his scent and whisper in his ear. "You didn't have to get me drunk.

While Biast didn't have to get me drunk for me to desire him more than anything right now, that didn't necessarily mean that this was right. Because, it wasn't. No matter how much I wanted Biast to take me to a Lust Room and finally have his way with me, I couldn't do that to Eros.

Despite everything, I climbed off him and grabbed his hand. "Follow me."

"Where are you taking me?" Biast said, following behind me with his barbed wire tail crawling up my thigh like it always did, touching me in places that it really, really shouldn't. Especially not when I was feeling this woozy.

"To find Eros, so he can watch," I said to him as if it was nothing. "If he agrees to it."

"Watch?"

I glanced back at him. "To watch you fuck me, because that's what you want to do, isn't it, Biast?" My lips curled into a small smile, the scent of his arousal drifting through my nostrils and filling me with pleasure. He didn't have to say it for me to know how much he had been craving this since the day we spent at that lava pit.

Wandering down the hallways with Biast in tow, I checked in my office, Eros's office, the kitchen, living room, and nearly all the castle rooms where him and Lucifer could've been. And, then, finally, I walked up to the bedroom.

"Lucifer," Eros said, voice drifting through our door.

"What?" Lucifer purred. "What is it, Eros? Feel too good?"

I gently nudged open the bedroom door and paused when I saw Eros sitting back on the bed and leaning against the headboard with a bulge in his pants. Lucifer sat next to him, his hand slipping down his abdomen closer and closer and closer to his belt buckle until Eros pushed him away. "Not until Dani comes back."

"What do we have here?" I asked. Tightening my hand around Biast's, I walked into the room with a big smirk on my face. "Lucifer and Eros in bed without inviting me?"

When Eros saw me, he shot up in the bed. "Dani—"

"Don't stop," I said to Lucifer who cracked a devilish smirk and peered toward Biast for a mere moment. I squeezed my thighs together and groaned internally. "Eros was just getting into it. And… it's turning me on."

"How was your dinne—" Eros started again.

I released Biast's hand, unzipped my dress, and climbed up onto the bed half-naked, not having the time nor the patience for questions. Instead, I grabbed Lucifer's hand and placed it right on Eros's bulge, my pussy tightening at the sight. At first, Eros tensed, then swallowed hard and relaxed back on the headboard as Lucifer stroked him.

"Biast is going to fuck me, you're going to watch, and Lucifer is going to make sure that you enjoy it," I said to Eros, stripping off my panties and knowing that—despite whether Eros liked Biast or not—he wouldn't pass up an opportunity to watch another demon fuck me.

Glancing over my shoulder, I curled my finger in Biast's direction. "Come here."

After crawling on the bed with me, Biast unfastened his pants, pushed them down to his knees, and shoved my upper body down against Eros. Before I could even prepare for him to bury himself inside, Biast rammed into me. I let out a loud moan, the pressure turning to pleasure within a moment.

"Fuuuck," Biast growled, grasping a fistful of my hair and yanking me back up—rough, just like I expected him to be. "You're so much tighter than I thought you'd be."

Lucifer unbuttoned Eros's pants and pulled out his thick,

veiny cock, fingers wrapping around the hilt. Eros tensed and blew out a deep breath, the way he always did when he liked something more than he should've. I tightened around Biast.

"Look at the way he fucking pounds into her pussy," Lucifer said into Eros's ear, stroking him faster and faster with every passing moment. Lucifer kissed Eros's neck and chuckled in his ear. "Feel her tits sway against your thighs, smell her arousal for him, watch all that pleasure on her face."

My pussy pulsed at the sight of Lucifer's hand wrapped around Eros. I both wanted Eros inside of me and didn't want Lucifer to stop. Just seeing it was going to make me come already, and it hadn't even been five minutes yet.

Biast slipped a hand around my throat and strummed his harsh fingers against it, his barbed tail wrapping around my abdomen, restricting it, and oddly making me feel... good. With the lust building inside of me, *everything* felt good.

I dug my fingers into Eros's thighs and moaned out, wanting him inside of me. He stared down at me, his eyes filled completely with dark madness. He parted his lips and furrowed his brows, and was just about to come on his stomach when I took him into my mouth and let him come inside of me as Lucifer continued to stroke what I couldn't fit.

Eros bucked his hips, his warm cum shooting out and sliding all the way down my throat. Biast curled his hands around my hips and grunted, pulling back on my hair and tugging me off Eros's cock, all his cum dripping out of my mouth. Reaching forward, Lucifer swiped some of cum off my chin and rubbed it against my clit.

I tightened around Biast, the pressure building so high in my core, and moaned out as I came all over him. Lucifer continued to touch my pussy until my legs gave out and I laid in Eros's lap with my ass up as Biast thrust into me one last time, pulled out, and came all over my back.

~

An hour later, I turned onto my side to face Biast, admiring the way that the wired tail had seemed to soften and curl onto his legs, the barbs not as sharp and pointy as they once were when he hadn't had a good release. "Now, I want my information about the woman who killed my mother."

Biast laid back in the bed and blew out a steady, controlled breath, his taut chest falling. "She's a member of my father's religion and has vowed to protect Hell from angels. From what I could gather, she's extremely strong and doesn't die easily—you might not even have the power to kill her as quickly as you have been killing demons. Her mission is to cleanse these lands of any purity, and she thought your mother was tainting the corrupt like your father. She blends in easily with humans, because she's half-human herself, and will gladly take on a mission to kill good humans or angels."

Balling my hands into fists, I let out a small growl. "Have you seen her?"

"No," Biast said. "Not for over a decade, maybe two at this point."

Eros rolled over behind me, placed his hand on my hip, and looked at Biast. "Do you know where she could be? Where does she hang out? Does your father know anything?"

"Sathanus is out of the equation," I said. "Biast is going to kill him."

Lucifer chuckled, toying with the end of one of his ice horns. "Kill him? Finally growing a backbone and not taking anymore of his shit. I give it to you. He's a bastard that I've wanted to kill for years, I couldn't imagine living with that fucking man."

"I don't know if I'm going to kill him yet," Biast said.

"You will," I said, leaning back and resting my head on the pillow. One day, Biast would get fed up with Sathanus calling him out, ruining his life, and putting him down, and that would be the end of Sathanus's rule.

Especially if Biast thought that this prophecy was about us and was true.

"Either way, whether you know where she is or not, it might not be beneficial for us to kill her just yet," Lucifer said.

Us.

Lucifer said *us*.

As if we were a team.

After Lucifer swiped a hand over his face, he leaned back on the bed. "She can help us in the coming war against Heaven. She may be someone who could potentially be our ally to kill some angels, especially if she's been doing it for centuries, millennium even."

I balled my hands into fists. "Why would I be allies with someone who killed my mother?"

"Because she might be able to help us."

"I don't need help."

"You don't know Mother," Lucifer said.

I glanced over at Eros with my brows furrowed. He shrugged. "He's right."

Teaming up with the woman who killed my mother? The woman who had it out for me too? Not only did that sound like a bad idea waiting to happen, but I couldn't do that. I had been out to avenge Mom's death, not team up with the demon who killed her just to win a war.

Biast placed his fingers on my stomach, and somehow all the rage inside of me seemed to dampen—just a little—as if he was sucking it out of me, because rage didn't sit well inside of a Lust demon, but a Wrath thrived off it.

I didn't know if it was selfish or sweet.

After blowing out a deep breath, I shut my eyes and hoped that I'd be able to get some sleep tonight. My cravings and desire had been quenched for now, and I hoped that it would be so later, instead of those nightmares haunting my dreams.

Yet even hours into the night, I found myself staring at the ceiling and admiring the way the pink moonlight glimmered against it. Eros brushed his knuckles against mine and hummed into my ear. "Are you still awake?"

I turned on my side to face him and placed a kiss on his lips as Biast and Lucifer slept on either side of us.

"How was your night?"

"In Wrath?" I asked, frowning. "It was fine. Sathanus talked a big game about killing me, but he didn't try anything. At least, Biast made it bearable." I glanced over his shoulder at Lucifer who was sound asleep. "What about you? Do you want to finally tell me about him?"

Eros sighed softly. "I've told you that we were together thousands of years ago, and when my parents kicked me out... he offered me a kingdom to sleep in."

"You have feelings for him," I said, clarifying. "Have you told him?"

Eros gazed out our bedroom window and sighed. "No, but I assume that he knows already. I just... I can't get myself to trust him again. Last time, I sacrificed everything for him: Heaven, love, a good life, and got screwed over. He's a good man but he lets his pride get too much in the way sometimes."

"That's why you want to keep him around," I said, brushing some hair off his forehead. "You don't want to get hurt again. You want to be able to see him everyday." And, while it would've made most people angry, I wasn't.

I loved Eros so much.

I just didn't want him to go behind my back like Trevon did. As long as Eros was open to me about what he wanted from Lucifer, I was fine with it. We *were* the Queen and King of the Kingdom of Lust. It was bound to happen sooner or later.

"Do *you* want to try to be with him too?" I asked.

Eros had pushed me to get together with Lucifer for such a long time and so hard too, it shocked me that he was hesitant. I thought for sure that this would be his way of getting closer to him again, but maybe it was his way of spending more time with Lucifer without feeling how he had before. I didn't blame him.

"We talked about this before," I continued. "Our kingdom is secure. Nobody will attack. You saw how they all acted in the meeting the other day. They might have been talking about taking my kingdom away but nobody directly suggested it, not even Sathanus. They were terrified that I'd lose control again. If you want to have a relationship with—"

"No," Eros said, shaking his head as soon as the words left my mouth. "We can get together... but... no. I can't have a relationship with him. Not now. I'm still... nervous about it all, if I'm honest with you, Dani. I don't want you to slip away either... What about Biast? Jasmine?"

"We're just friends," I admitted truthfully. I knew that when people said that, most people actually meant that they had raging feelings for each other, and I may have some toward both of them... but I didn't know what they meant and I wasn't ready to act on *any* of those intimate and emotional urges yet. I had Eros and would adjust with life with Lucifer—maybe—too. "But... I do feel a pull toward them both. I'm just not ready for that yet. We have too many other things to worry about right now."

"When you're ready, you'll tell me?" he asked, brows furrowed.

I gently stroked his face. "Yes, I will, but I want you to know that you... you are the only thing that I'm completely sure of, Eros." I leaned in close to him. "I love you with everything that I have and will continue to love you endlessly."

CHAPTER 19

"You killed my son!" an Envy screamed at me, green tears racing down her cheeks.

I stood in the center of the white marble arena that my crowning took place in, the once lively audience all now mere corpses, the rotten stench drifting through my nose. My heart raced at the sight and at the smell, never having thought that this was what hell could have done to me.

"My baby!" a woman shouted, collapsing onto her hands and knees and pulling a carcass into her lap. She drew her finger down his horns made of ice and sobbed hysterically, the colosseum filling with screaming, weeping, and undeniable sorrow.

While I wanted to shout out the words "I'm sorry," to the crowd, I couldn't quite get them past my lips. I wasn't sorry for what I did. I was defending my crown and my title. I would never have touched the people who obeyed, who accepted, who thought of me as equal even if I had grown up as human and was part angel.

I was the Queen.

Yet I still felt the pain of a million subjects, ripping apart my insides and butchering my heart. My angel wanted to reach out to all these families and comfort them, fly around Hell and fix everything. But Hell didn't need fixing. Hell was perfect the way it was.

People weren't meant to be all holy and good.

People had faults. People had desires. People were bad sometimes.

It made the good times worth it.

Suddenly the sea of sobs engulfed me, the demons drowning me, trembling me, suffocating me. I reached my hands up and grabbed them, pulling them down—or at least trying to pull me back up. Though their hands were all over my body, tearing into me, Minseok was the man standing above me.

"It's time, Dani," he said. "Let go of your pain and follow me."

When he extended a hand toward me, I took it only to pull myself out of the mess. And once I was out, I dropped it and pushed him away, the corruption running through my veins and making me feel too good. All this time I was spending with Eros, Lucifer, and Biast was really going to my head.

But I found a family down here that I didn't want to lose.

Turning on my heel, I found myself spinning back into a nightmare of the past with Javier, trapping me in his Lust Room that I hadn't returned to since that dreadful night. He shut the door behind us and looked over his shoulder. "You're not jealous of the Lust whores, are you? Because that's what you are now, Dani. A Lust whore who sleeps with whoever she wants to, who uses people for their bodies, and who destroys lives."

I balled my hands into fists, not willing to be that innocent girl he pushed around anymore. "I'm not jealous of any demon from Lust. Being a whore isn't shameful. You fuck whoever you had wanted all the time and you find no shame in it, do you?" I stalked closer to him, forcing him to step back to his king-size oak bed.

Javier stopped when his thighs met the mattress and began to unbutton his shirt. "I don't, which is why I brought you here, Queen*. I want to finally get a taste of you, and this time you'll let me because... you can't control yourself no matter how hard you try to. You'll* *always..." He curled a finger around my brown hair and tugged. "Always want more."*

I balled my hands into fists, wanting to protest, but not having it in me.

Because he was right.

Not only did I love lust. But I was a greedy bastard too.

"Now," Javier said, cracking a smirk. "Take off your dress."

Wrath from the audacity to talk to me this way, pride that I had stood up to him for once, and lust to taste his cold and lifeless lips again ran through my veins. That's what I felt right here, right now. Fucking Javier—even in a dream—wouldn't make me feel better, but if I killed him now, maybed he'd finally shut his mouth.

So, I reached behind me and unzipped my dress, letting it fall to the ground and stepped toward him to put him into a trance. I needed complete control of him, if I wanted to finally sever him from my mind. He widened his eyes as if he didn't expect me to actually listen to his command, but then slouched onto the bed and relaxed.

Unlike last time, I wasn't doing this to get back at Eros, I wasn't doing this because I was in pain, I wasn't doing this to make myself feel better. I was doing this because I was in control. Not only was this my dream, but this was my head that a dead man had been fucking with. I would take no more suffering from him.

Javier grabbed my hips and pulled me on top of him so I straddled his waist, his talons curling into my flesh and nearly piercing through the skin, just as Biast's had last night. "One minute you're lying in my brother's bed, and the next you're wet for me," he said. Javier left sloppy, rough kisses down my neck, then my chest, capturing my nipple into his mouth. "What do you want, Dani?" he asked, biting down hard. "Tell me what you want."

I snaked my hand around his throat and smirked down at him, lust rushing through me at the sight of his lips and at the thought of killing him yet again and ending this madness for good this time. My heart pumped with excitement as I leaned down slightly. "I want to kiss you."

Dipping my head, I captured his lips with mine and refused to let him go, because I missed the taste of his pepper-y mouth and the power I felt when I straddled his waist and ended his pathetic life.

My mind fogged. My thoughts slowed. My tongue traced the fangs in his mouth.

Feeding myself off his rage and desire, sipping it out and drinking it down, I claimed his soul inside of me once more. Javier would always be special to me. He had been the first soul I captured, the first time I ever felt true power.

Yet, when he fell limp under me and I pulled away from our kiss, it didn't make me feel better. It quenched my thirst for just a moment, but then it returned, raging harder and hotter, bubbling inside of me and refusing to let me stop now.

I stood up, wanting and needing more, and glanced into the mirror in Javier's Lust Room.

Mom stood on the other side, frowning at me for what I had become. "What happened to you, Dani?" she whispered, her soft hair drawn into curls and her angelic face tight with sorrow. "What happened to my baby girl? The one I'd take to the skating rink and walk down the city streets with?"

Tremendous guilt washed over me, my heart clenching.

I desperately wanted to tell her that she wasn't here anymore, that she died with her.

But, again, I couldn't get the words out of my mouth. I was a monster, but deep down I was still her girl, I still had those memories, I still cried because I missed my mom so much. And killing all these people tore families apart, just like the red-eyed woman had torn mine apart. I wasn't any better than her, but I wasn't any worse either.

My life had turned into a juxtaposition that I couldn't escape, because I felt both great happiness and great sorrow for everything I had done these past few weeks.

"Let me show you what your demon has caused," Mom said to me. She disappeared, and I reached for the mirror, not ever wanting to let her go. But instead of grasping the glass, I found myself stumbling through it into my old apartment with Trevon lying on the couch.

A layer of his skin seared off, his flesh red and blotchy, he stared at me with wide and glossy eyes. "Dani," he whispered. "Dani, help me. I can't take this pain any longer..." He glanced toward three knifes on the living room table. "If you don't help... I'll... I'll... have to end this all myself. The pain is unbearable." Trevon reached for the largest knife of the three and held it to his neck. "Help me, Dani."

"Don't do that, Trevon," I pleaded with him. "Don't... please, don't."

"You've taken too long, Dani. I've been calling for you to help me for days. You never come."

And before I could stop him, he slit his throat.

CHAPTER 20

I shot up in the bed and screamed at the top of my lungs for Trevon to stop slitting his throat. Once peacefully lying next to me, Biast sat up and lengthened his claws, one arm around my waist and the other ready to break someone's face. Eros grabbed my hand and rubbed it gently from beside me. And good 'ole Lucifer opened one eye, grumbled to himself about me waking his beauty sleep, and turned in the bed.

"What's going on?" Biast asked, eyes blazing like Wrath's lava pits.

"I… I…" I jumped out of bed and pulled on some clothes suitable for Earth. "I have to go see Trevon. He's hurting. I saw it in my nightmare, and I've been ignoring him because I have so much going on and I don't know what to do and all this pain and—"

Eros placed a hand on my shoulder and grasped my jaw to force me to look up at him. "Slow down and breathe, Dani," Eros demanded, staring at me with those lovely green eyes. "I'll have Jasmine make you tea or a Passion—"

"No, I don't have time for that," I said, trying to push him away. "If you don't want to come, you don't have to. But I have to go. Now." After pulling and tugging on his hands to try to get out of his grip, I sighed and flared my nostrils, glaring up at him. "Let me go."

"Calm down," Eros said sternly, fingers strumming against my jaw. "Calm."

I took deep breath after deep breath to relax and found nothing working, until I looked up into his soft eyes and finally slumped my shoulders. We might've laid with other people, but Eros was one of the only demons who could ever calm me down this much.

Leaning forward, I placed my forehead against his and wrapped him into a hug. "Can you come with me to Earth? Trevon is hurting, and I need to help him. I don't want to go alone, because…" Something deep inside me stirred, and for the first time I realized that I didn't hear those voices in my head anymore. They were gone for now.

Javier was gone.

All the constant voices telling me to kill had vanished.

And I had to live with all the pain I caused.

"Because why, Dani?" Eros said softly, voice barely above a whisper.

"Because I can't do it alone. I'm afraid I'll break."

Eros tucked some hair behind my ear and smiled. "That wasn't too hard to admit, was it?" he asked with a half smile. "We're in this together. Where you go, I go. What happens to you, what happens to me, it's our problem to deal with."

Intertwining my hand in his, I pulled him closer to me. "Thank you."

"Alright, enough with all the lovey-dovey shit," Lucifer said, who instead of sleeping was tugging on his pants from our bedside. "Are we going to Earth or not?" He looked back at Biast who still laid on the bed and stared at me with those blazing red eyes. "Care to join us?"

My eyes widened slightly, and I stared at him hopefully.

Biast shuffled out of the bed and tugged a shirt over his head. "It's better than heading back to Wrath to see my father."

"Should we invite Jasmine too?" Lucifer asked, a chilling smile on his pale face. "Everyone that Dani has ever slept with in the same room together for once in her entire life?"

I let out a laugh, grabbed Eros's hand, and headed for the door. "We'll save Jasmine the awkwardness of meeting Trevon while he's nearly dying," I said, the words supposed to come out lighthearted, but this was far from funny and far from light.

This was fucking heavy.

~

3AM darkness encompassed the city, the bus lines deserted for the night, a couple lights flickered on in the skyscrapers above, and my three demons followed me down the slushy sidewalks to Maria's apartment building.

Using the keycard I still had to gain access into the building, I snuck them in and furiously tapped on the *Door Close* button in the elevator. My stomach tightened into knots at the thought of walking into Maria's apartment and seeing Trevon dead.

When the doors opened, I sprinted to Maria's apartment and banged on her front door, needing someone to answer now. One moment passed, then another, then Maria opened the door holding a butcher knife in her hands. After realizing it was me, she rolled her eyes and placed it down onto the side table. "What is going on? Why are you here at three in the morning?"

"Trevon." I stepped into the foyer and hurried to the living room couch.

Just like in my dream, three knives laid on the center table, one knife covered in red goo. I shrieked as Trevon called out my name in his sleep and collapsed next to him, clutching his burning neck to stop blood. And when my hand wrapped too tightly around him, Trevon blinked his eyes open and grabbed it hard.

"What are you doing, Dani?" Trevon asked, shoving me back slightly. "Trying to kill me?"

I glanced down at my hands not seeing any blood and furrowed my brows. "You didn't… slit your throat?" I whispered, looking back at his neck to see nothing but peeling skin, red flesh, and more bubbles than yesterday.

"I didn't slit my throat," Trevon said, voice hoarse and raspy. He went to grab at his throat again, but the skin on his hand cracked and blood gushed out of it. "But, fuck, this shit hurts too much. I wish I could."

Slapping him hard on the chest, I scolded, "Don't you ever say that."

Eros tossed him a towel to clean up the blood.

"What's with the knives then?" I asked.

"I got hungry and made a PBJ sandwich," Trevon said, sitting up on the couch and grabbing the towel to wipe the blood off his hand, then looking back at me. "Is that wrong?"

Rolling my eyes, I sat back on my ass and blew out a deep breath. "Fuck, Trevon, don't scare me like that. I thought you killed yourself. I was so worried about you that I towed all three of these guys here with me."

Maria lingered by the door with that knife in her hand, eyeing Biast. "Isn't he the guy you told me about who possessed Trevon before?"

"Long story," Biast grumbled, taking a seat on the couch opposite of Trevon.

Eros sat next to him. "Where's Zane? I thought Dani said he was staying here with you?"

Maria hiked her thumb back to her bedroom. "He is."

Kneeling beside Trevon, I grabbed the nearly empty bottle of lotion, pulled up the back of his shirt, and spread some cream across his peeling and bubbling back. I winced when my fingers glided against some softer than usual skin, fingers dipping into what used to be muscle but now felt a bit liquidy and gooey.

When I spread the cream across one of the bubbles, it burst under the slightest pressure, pink and red pus spraying out. Lucifer yanked me back by the collar just before it could splatter on me. Trevon howled and doubled over, spitting up blood onto Maria's white carpet.

"I knew I shouldn't have gotten white carpets after last time," she said, grabbing him a bucket to puke blood into.

And, before I knew it, all the bubbles in his back were bursting and splattering against the couch, the pus scattering everywhere and the blood pouring from Trevon's mouth. I backed up into Lucifer, my chest tight and my eyes wide in fear. "What the fuck is happening? I thought that this stuff was supposed to make him better?"

"Angels don't react to this stuff the same way that demons do," Biast said, examining the lotion tube.

I cut my gaze to him. "You're not helping."

With a brown paling face, Trevon clutched his stomach and doubled forward as if he couldn't hold himself up anymore. Before he could smack into the bin of blood and send it against the carpet, Eros caught him by the shoulders and laid him back onto the couch.

"What are we going to do?" I whispered to the guys, wanting Trevon to sleep a bit. It was sure of a lot better than him puking up blood and getting himself sick. I pushed away the tears forming in my eyes. "The doctor isn't helping him at all."

"He'll die," Biast said blatantly.

And I knew that if he didn't get help soon, he really would. Even the best doctors in all of Hell couldn't fix him. Though there was one person who could, I just didn't want to talk to her or get her involved in the slightest.

"I have to go to Heaven to visit Mother," I said, knowing that I shouldn't. But I didn't want Trevon to die this painful death.

Though he cheated on me with Javier, I still loved the man as a friend. We had spent all our lives growing up together, and to see him in such pain hurt me.

"Mother will try to control you. She promises people like you a stress-free life, but really she traps people in a prison. She'll try to convince you to stay too," Biast said, eyes fiery lava pits. "You'd be stupid to trust her."

"I don't trust her, but she's our only hope."

"Why don't you just let the man die?" Biast asked.

"He's my friend." I glanced down at Trevon, remembering all the times we spent together and all the memories that we made. It was stupid, but Trevon was my piece of humanity that I had left. If he died, I feared that I'd tip over the edge like I had at the crowning ceremony.

Eros grabbed my hand and pulled me closer to him. "I can't fuckng lose you, Dani."

"You're not going to lose me. I'll take him up there and come right back down."

"Let her go," Lucifer said, sitting down on the bloody couch next to Trevon and waving his hand dismissively. "Don't listen to Eros, and make sure you tell Mother that her good *friend* Luci says hi."

Eros intertwined our fingers, a strand of his brown hair lying across his forehead. "Promise that you'll come back for me and for your kingdom," he said against my lips. "I need you more than anything in this world, Dani."

Pulling my hands out of his, I gently grasped his face and nodded. "I promise you. I'll be back."

After convincing Eros, Lucifer, and Biast to bring Trevon to the ice skating rink for me, I sat on the bench with Trevon and gently rested my hand on his. My three demon *lovers* had departed for

Hell fifteen minutes ago, and I had been anxiously waiting for Minseok to show up. He never told me how to contact him, just to come here.

Two familiar voices drifted through the darkness of the city, shadows approaching from the pathway to my left. The ice skating rink didn't actually open for the next few hours, the gates locked with thick chains. Whoever it was must've jumped the fence.

Dr. U and Kasey walked down the pathway to the rink, Dr. U's arm curled around Kasey's, both smiling and laughing with each other. I sat up on the bench next to a nearly dead Trevon and smiled at how Dr. U looked. I might've not been on the best of terms with Kasey but I was glad that she not only saved Dr. U but made her laugh again.

"Dani," Dr. U said, finally noticing me. "What are you doing here?"

When they walked over to me, I gave them my best smile. "Waiting for someone."

"Who?" Kasey asked, dropping her arm and grasping Dr. U's hand.

Dr. U glanced down at Trevon and gasped, placing a hand to her heart, the veins against her pale skin a dark black. Kasey's blood still rushed through her veins, the demon inside Dr. U must've been growing by the day. One night soon, she'd transform into an unruly demon with black eyes and a lust for more.

"What happened to Trevon?" she asked me, brows furrowed.

"He's..." I started, wanting to tell them that he was half-angel. But I didn't fully trust Kasey anymore. If she found out about him, she could damn well try to kill him herself and hurt me for good. "He's just sick. I'm waiting for someone to heal him."

"In a dark ice skating rink?" Kasey asked.

"Yes," I said, clenching my jaw and staring at the glint of moonlight on the ice.

"You can tell us if something is wrong," Dr. U said, sitting next to me.

"Nothing is wrong."

"Dani…" Kasey started.

"Nothing. Is. Wrong."

Kasey stared at me with wide eyes, grabbed Dr. U's arm, and hauled her up with her. "We should get going. It's obvious that Dani doesn't want us here," Kasey said, and it fucking hurt because I always wanted Dr. U by my side. Just not Kasey as much anymore.

"If you need me, you know where you can find me, Dani," Dr. U said, giving me her best smile. She looked as if she wanted to pull me into a hug, but decided against it and turned back toward Kasey. "Why don't we just go back to my place?"

I watched them disappear down the path and frowned. This better not be for nothing.

CHAPTER 21

Another thirty minutes passed, and I found myself wondering if Minseok would actually meet me here. It wasn't like a goody-two-shoes like him to break curfew and sneak into a no-trespassing area during the late hours of the night, but I needed to see Mother, now.

I didn't want to talk to him about meeting her. I didn't *want* to meet her at all. But this wasn't for me and wasn't for my kingdom down in Hell. This was for Trevon, the man who I once loved, and for Mom, the woman I missed more and more every day of my life. I needed to know what really happened with Mom and why Mother wouldn't let her back into Heaven when she needed her the most.

Suddenly in the middle of the night, white clouds coasted over the rink and what looked to be marble stairs descended from them to the ice beside me. Minseok drifted down the stairs, toes barely grazing against the ground.

"You're here?" Minseok asked. "Even when it says no trespassing?"

"I don't have to follow the rules like you do."

Minseok set one foot upon the land, winced, and then stood before me, detracting his wings. He looked between Trevon and me, and frowned. "What would you like to discuss?"

"I want to meet with Mother," I said.

"That's wonderful! I'll let her know. We can set som—"

"I want to meet her now. I don't have time to wait. Trevon is getting worse, and… my memories of killing are getting the best of me. I need to know if there is a cure for both of us. I don't want this to control me for the rest of my life."

Minseok beamed at me with blazing white eyes. "You may be hurting for what you did to all those demons, but Mother doesn't see that as a betrayal in her eyes. She's all forgiving of those who eliminate the demons from the world." He walked around me, barely looking at Trevon, and brushed his fingers against my shoulder. "I can see that you want to repent and be forgiven for your sins. Mother will forgive you for everything. She'll accept you into her open arms and not hold any of your mistakes against you."

Biting back the damn annoyance from talk about Mother already, I forced a smile. "Okay, let's go," I whispered, hoping that I would be able to heal Trevon and leave without a scratch. Though something inside of me told me that I wouldn't be able to leave at all, that this was far from the right decision, that I should've let Trevon die.

"Are you sure?" Minseok asked, taking Trevon in his arms and elongating his wings.

I grabbed him by the collar and pulled him closer. "Bring me to Heaven, now."

"Yes, ma'am." Minseok nodded to the marble steps and urged me onto them. "Use your wings and fly up them. They're too tall and there are far too many for a human to just walk up them. Be like the angels. Fly, Dani, fly."

Closing my eyes, I took a deep breath and thought back to

when Minseok taught me how to use my wings. I focused on the center of my back, a pain shooting through my muscle, and felt wings extend out of me and pulling me off the ground.

Minseok beamed at me and urged me toward the marble steps. Toes just barely grazing against each step, I found myself floating up them with Minseok behind me. I continued up and up and up until the city that once surrounded me turned into thick white clouds.

"Keep going," Minseok said from behind me, still carrying Trevon in his arms.

About a hundred steps later, we came to two pearl posts with a glowing gate that was perched on top of an impalpable cloud. An attached golden fence stretched on for miles and miles in either direction until it disappeared into the sky.

My stomach tightened at the thought of finally entering into Heaven for the first time ever. Mom must've been here for thousands of years, memorized this place like the back of her hand, because whenever she used to tell me stories of her father up in this celestial place, she described these gates and these feathery clouds almost perfectly.

When we stepped onto the cloud, two angels with wings almost as grand as mine pulled the gates open for us. I swallowed hard and stepped into Mother's home, unsure if this was a ploy to get me alone or if she would actually help Trevon. But she was my only hope.

A line of human souls, who seemed to be waiting to be judged and accepted into Heaven, extended from the gates to the hundred golden hills to an enormous Cathedral. Minseok floated past the human souls with Trevon in his arms, and I followed.

"Why does Heaven have gates?" I asked him, glancing over my shoulder at the people we passed who stared in awe at us, then solely at my blackened feathers. Little did they know that angels weren't the only creatures to come to Heaven.

Minseok slowed down his pace to fly closer, almost too close. "To keep demons out."

"Not to keep angels in?" I asked, watching the way a confused expression crossed his face as if he never contemplated it before. Then he shook his head and laughed. "Not at all. Mother doesn't mind if we leave Heaven, especially if we come back every night."

"And if you don't come back every night? What happens then?"

Continuing past the humans, Minseok shrugged. "Nobody knows, and no angel dares to find out either. We would never even think about disobeying Mother's orders like that. She is too good to us."

We continued on across Heaven's golden hills, moving closer and closer to the Cathedral. Angels with pure white wings glanced over at me, narrowing their eyes at my black and dark wings, signalling that I wasn't one of them, but something corrupt and evil.

The Cathedral bells rang two times, their loud and low chimes echoing through all of Heaven. Minseok jerked his head up, gazing down the path toward the Cathedral which could be seen from everywhere in Heaven. Mother must've been inside and always watching over them.

When the Cathedral doors opened, the sounds of a hundred angel wings flapping exited the grand church and dispersed throughout Heaven, eyes glowing white and facial features soft like a child. I balled my hands into fists, both enjoying the feeling of being here and loathing it, because while it felt natural, it also felt fucking absurd.

As we reached the front of the line at the Cathedral doors, I gazed down a long pathway of golden apple trees that I must've taken Eros the morning after my crowning ceremony. Instead of following Minseok into the church, I found myself walking down the pathway of trees and smiling.

Red apples hung from the branches, and I reached up to grab one. Before I could pull the bob off the tree, Minseok grabbed my wrist and pulled it away. "What are you doing?" he scolded. "Taking fruit from the trees is forbidden."

"But—"

"If Mother finds you taking one, she'll punish you," he said to me, tugging me back toward the Cathedral and in through the side doors. Four rows wide and at least fifty pews long, the Cathedral was filled with peaceful chatter from humans waiting to be judged. People of all nationalities and all religions stood together in a line, their words tender and endearing.

The glass walls, stained with the finest reds, blues, and yellows, climbed at least a hundred feet in the air. An enormous white-stained glass door in the back of the room opened, an angel with small wings floating out of it. Another human walked in and shut the door behind him.

"Is Mother there?" I asked Minseok.

A moment later, the door opened again and that same human departed with a set of small white wings. I found myself balling my hands into fists and glaring at the door with such angst. Something told me that this was the wrong decision, that I shouldn't be here, that I should take Trevon and leave now.

But Minseok was already floating down the aisle to the grand white door.

"Mother," he called before I could stop him.

My stomach tightened as a celestial being floated out of the room with a golden cross around her neck, coiled curls crowning her brown face, and a thin white tunic covering her body. Unlike Minseok, I stood straighter and lifted my gaze to stare right into her eyes, so she knew that I meant business and that she didn't terrify me.

"Dani," she said, voice soft like the wind. "You've come to meet me."

"I'm here so you can treat Trevon," I said. "One of your angels."

"You're one of my angels too, Dani," she paused and smiled. "I'm so happy to finally get to see you. You're everything I pictured you'd be and more. This is a wonderful surprise." She glanced at the other humans behind us. "Your souls will be judged tomorrow. Please, go into Heaven and rest under the apple trees."

The humans started filing out of the enormous cathedral and into Heaven. I stood back and watched them through the stained glass, heart thrashing against my ribcage. I didn't want to be here with her alone, because… it didn't feel right.

Something was telling me to run.

Examining the room, I looked for a quick escape but all the doors were guarded by large celestial warriors who kept their gaze focused on me and only me. I inched closer to Minseok, forming a plan in case things went south.

"It's beautiful, isn't it?" Mother asked me.

Yeah, beautiful, that's exactly what I was thinking about.

Definitely not how to escape.

"Amazing." I offered her a tightlipped smile. "Now, I'd like you to help my friend and one of *your* children who is dying in Minseok's arms."

"Of course. Of course." Mother moved closer to me and brushed her fingers against my cheek, her touch cold and surprisingly uninviting to me, then she motioned for Minseok to move forward. "Bring him here, Minseok."

Within the depths of my mind, demons seethed at me, warning me out of Heaven, out of this church, and out of sight from Mother for good. Yet Javier—who I thought I had ended for good—rang the loudest. *"I don't need to be a fallen angel to know that Mother will do nothing for Trevon."*

Just like Javier used Trevon for his own selfish reasons, Mother did too.

She didn't really care about my ex-boyfriend. She cared about protecting her rule.

So, I grabbed Minseok's arm and pushed him behind me.

Mother grasped my jaw lightly in her hand. "I know that you don't trust me. I know that you're hurting. I can feel it. All those corrupt souls in your mind, eating away at any of the goodness that you have left..." She offered me a soft smile. "Live in Heaven. Be with me and the rest of your brothers and sisters. I will forgive everything you've done and erase all those terrible memories and voices plaguing your mind."

Before she could move even closer, I stepped back. "If you wanted me here, you would've accepted my mother when she asked for your help."

"Oh dear. Is that what those demons in Hell told you? That I didn't want you? Don't like foolish men like Eros and Lucifer sway your decisions. Think for yourself," she said, ignoring me. "If I didn't want you here, you wouldn't be here now."

I pursed my lips. I loved Eros, and Lucifer was a good guy too. But they weren't the ones swaying my decisions. I had been pondering over my mother's death for years, wondering what the fuck killed her. Now that I knew the truth, I wasn't going to let Mother ignoring her pleas slide.

"I'm an anomaly to you. I'm a demon. I'm the strongest in all of Hell. You want me here and under your control because you fear me." I stared at her straight in the eye. "Because I'll be your destruction and you know it, just like you knew Beliel would be yours, which is why you sent her away."

"You know nothing about Belial." Mother straightened her back and looked down upon me. "Nothing about the treacherous sins she committed against me. You will never understand why I sent her away... but let me show you."

Suddenly, she grabbed hold of my jaw and pulled me close, memories that weren't mine flooding through my mind. I went to grab her wrist to pull her away but she was stronger than I expected, and I could do nothing but stand there and relive the experience of thousands upon thousands of years ago.

"Every day we all sacrifice. Every day we all follow the commandments. I have created these ten simple actions so you can live your best life, so you stay faithful to who you truly are, my children." Mother lifted her arms, gesturing to the church full of angels but never taking her eyes off of a woman with almost bare wings, the woman I had only heard stories of, the woman Belial. "Have I not rewarded you for your incredible sacrifices?"

Everyone bowed their heads. "You have, Mother," the room said in unison.

But Lucifer didn't speak a word.

In the midst of the silence, Belial cleared her throat. "You have not." She held out her hands. "I sacrifice too much to be offered only this. I want freedom. We want freedom."

Everyone gasped, but Mother held up her hand, and everyone became silent again. "Please step forward, Belial."

Belial didn't hesitate to exit her pew. She walked down the aisle, her wings shredding the last of her shriveled and stained feathers. And when Belial made it to the altar, she didn't bow her head. Instead she glared with so much hatred that it tainted the Cathedral's aura.

"What are the ten commandments, my children?" she asked, never dropping eye contact from Belial.

Like a choir, they repeated the commandments back to her as I watched, hundreds of angels blindly speak back to her, even Eros and Lucifer. Though Eros couldn't say the tenth rule, Lucifer sneered as the tenth and only commandment passed his lips and his wife's arm wrapped tighter around him.

Thou shall not covet.

Covet. Had Eros desired Lucifer in Heaven, behind Lucifer's wife's back? Was that where their love affair began?

Mother broke eye contact and gazed at her children. "I have given the Angel Belial many chances and she has disrespected me," she said. "I will gift her one more." Her eyes softened, and she reached for Belial's cheek. "I want to see you thrive, my child."

Belial smacked her hand away.

"Belial doesn't seem to want another chance." She shook her head, and, for a moment, a grave expression crossed her face. "She wants a life like this." The clouds underneath the glass beneath our feet turned a murky black like the smoke from the human's fires. No white, no light, just darkness engulfing them.

Outside the red stained-glass wall, a herd of bulls—each with sharp horns pointed straight at the glass—sprinted in the direction of the church. They crashed into the edges of it, the windows shaking but not breaking. Drool and foam oozed from their mouths.

Outside the purple stained-glass window, creatures with far too pronounced features, hips too wide, breasts too big, bottoms too round, and eyes too seductive drew people in. They danced with each other and made love to each other—all together, not even ashamed. They looked to be human yet looks were deceiving because no human in their right mind would be so sinful to these angels.

Lucifer locked his gaze on the blue window. Outside the blue stained-glass window, creatures that looked to be a mix of human, angel, and bull sat atop of thousands of barrels of gold, throwing the poor to the side like they were rats. They ate more food than they needed, their bellies big.

Belial didn't look frightened like the rest of the angels did.

"I will have to send her away," Mother said.

"To freedom," Belial said. With a wide grin on her face and an evil glint in her eye, she faced the church and fell to her knees. Her wings were now just a skeleton, each brittle bone decaying rather rapidly.

The cross around Mother's neck glowed with a white aura, and when she removed it, it lengthened into something far more dangerous. A blade. With white edges that glowed with a blinding brightness, she held the smallest end in her hand.

Eros grabbed Lucifer's hand.

Mother grabbed the center of Belial's wings. "Once you repent, you will be allowed back into our wonderful Heaven."

Belial gazed at them. "I will never repent. I want freedom."

There was more to the memory, I could tell. But Mother stopped it there because she only wanted to show me how poorly Belial treated her and how many chances Mother had given her. But I wasn't buying it one freaking bit.

"If you're so gracious, what happened to my mother? Why didn't you let her back into Heaven after she had been with my father, after she loved him for years, after… after she had me—one of your *children*?"

The word sounded sour on my tongue. She was no mother. She was a monster. If she showed me all the bad things demons had done in this world, all the times she supposedly gave them chances, I still would never trust her. She had broken that trust decades before I came up here to speak with her. She had been stuck in her ways for thousands of years.

Nothing would change her.

Especially not me.

The only thing that could change the way we lived was war.

"You are not listening to me, Dani. Just like your mother didn't," Mother said. "Your mother betrayed me. Your mother left me, left Heaven, left all her brothers and sisters behind to spend a life with a demon, the one man I told her to avoid."

"And when she needed you the most, *when I needed you the most,* you denied her."

"She made her decision."

"But she didn't make mine." I balled my hands into fists. "If you are who you say you are, if every child is born without the mistakes of their families weighing them down, you should've accepted me into Heaven when my mother pleaded with you to take me. Instead you ignored me for more than twenty years, while demons slowly slithered into my life."

"I suggest you correct your tone with me," Mother responded, not even addressing her wrongdoing. And I hated her so much more for that. Gods weren't all holy and good. Gods like her were dangerous.

"Dani," Minseok said, staring at me with wide fearful eyes. He shook his head as if to tell me to stop talking right now, but I wasn't holding back any longer. Mother wanted war. It was probably all part of her plans to keep me up here. This had been a long time coming.

While leaving Heaven now wouldn't get me answers, I'd rather live with questions for eternity, then listen to Mother spew lies and hatred about my kind. We might've been demons. We might've been monsters to her. But we didn't pretend to be all holy and gracious as we trapped angels in a forbidden Heaven.

"There is no turning back now, no apologizing. My mother made her decision." I looked Mother right in the eye, feeling the darkness overtake me. Voices of those I'd killed swirled inside of me. My vision went dark for a mere moment. "And you made yours."

Surrendering control to the force inside of me, I grabbed Minseok by the throat and sunk my charcoal black claws into his neck. Almost instinctively, Minseok dropped Trevon's body on the glass floor, nearly making it shatter. My heart broke at the thought of leaving Trevon here, but it was him or all of Hell.

Hopefully, Mother would heal him a bit so he didn't die up here and under her watch. She wouldn't want any one of her angels finding out about another death that she could've prevented, so she would. *I hoped.*

When Mother thrust forward toward me, I leapt into the air

and let my wings spring out from behind me, more of my feathers blackening by the moment. Minseok grasped for his throat, yet I tugged him closer, closed my eyes, and pressed my lips to his, taking enough of his soul to break him. Minseok struggled underneath me, but I held him close and dodged as many holy attacks from other angels in here as possible.

A beam of light shot through the air, and seared right through part of my left wing, incinerating it completely. For a moment, I fell through the air, but I regained my composure and held Minseok steady. Bringing an angel to Hell was a sure way to end his life, giving him a slow and painful death just like Trevon. I didn't want to end Minseok's because he had been sweet to me, but I needed to get out of here and this was the only way.

Minseok must've been one of her most powerful angels, but even the strongest angels could be tempted. And I planned to do just that. If I broke him even further, he might even give me information about how to win the war.

Flying right through a red-stained glass window, I let the glass shatter around me and made a bee-line for the golden fence. Another beam of light shot through the air from Mother, searing the bottom of my right wing. My body fell for a moment, and I clutched Minseok even harder.

A swarm of angels followed me through Heaven, shooting attack after attack in my direction and all being led by a furious god. Instead of heading toward the gate, I flew to the golden fence and easily thrust my body between two of the glowing bars. Minseok shrieked underneath me, his skin melting away almost immediately.

All the angels stopped before they made contact with the fence and stared down at us. I had been right. That gate wasn't to keep demons out, but to keep the angels trapped in Heaven for as long as Mother needed them to be.

"You will pay for this, Dani Asmodeus!" Mother screamed,

throwing bolt after bolt of light down. Angels prepared at the borders with golden spears and bows, shooting them at me.

Dodging golden arrows and light strikes, I flew down the steps and through the air toward Hell. "This is war, Mother! I hope you are prepared."

To Be Continued...

ALSO BY DESTINY DIESS

The Marking: https://books2read.com/u/mgzEMq/

ABOUT THE AUTHOR

Destiny Diess is an international bestselling author of paranormal romance. With over 28 million story reads online, Destiny enjoys writing novels about werewolves, demons, and gods. She was born and raised in Westerly, RI, and now resides in Pittsburgh.

ACKNOWLEDGMENTS

Credit to Amelia Rodriguez for the suggestion of the name Minseok!

Made in the USA
Coppell, TX
29 March 2021

52609957R00094